T0163186

PENGUIN BOOKS

HAVE I GOT SOMETHING TO TELL YOU

An internationally recognized author, Malachi Edwin Vethamani is a fictionist, poet, editor, critic, bibliographer, and academic. His publications include five collections of poems: *The Seven O'clock Tree* (2022), *Love and Loss* (2022), *Rambutan Kisses* (2022), *Life Happens* (2017), and *Complicated Lives* (2016). *Coitus Interruptus and Other Stories* (2018) was his debut collection of stories. His stories have also been published in *Queer Southeast Asia Literary Journal* (2020), *Ronggeng-Ronggeng: Malaysian Short Stories* (2020), *Creative Flight Literary Journal* (2020), *Business Mirror* (2018), *Lakeview International Journal of Literature and Arts* (2017), and the 'Literary Page', *New Straits Times* (1995, 1996).

A theatrical adaptation of three of his stories from *Coitus Interruptus and Other Stories* were reworked as monologues and performed as 'Love Matters' by Playpen Performing Arts Trust in Mumbai in 2017 and 2018. His short story 'Best Man's Kiss' was reworked into a short play for an event called 'Inqueerable' organized by Queer Ink in Mumbai in 2019. He has edited five anthologies of Malaysian Literature in English: *The Year of the Rat and Other Poems* (2022), *Malaysian Millennial Voices* (2021), *Malchin Testament: Malaysian Poems* (2018), *Ronggeng-Ronggeng: Malaysian Short Stories* (2020). The Malaysian Publishers Association awarded *Malchin Testament: Malaysian Poems* the Malaysian Book Award 2020 for the

English Language category and *Ronggeng-Ronggeng: Malaysian Short Stories* was shortlisted for the Malaysian Book Award 2023 for the English Language category. He is Emeritus Professor with the University of Nottingham and Founding Editor of *Men Matters Online Journal.*

ADVANCE PRAISE FOR
HAVE I GOT SOMETHING TO TELL YOU

'Malachi Edwin Vethamani's twenty short stories span half a century of Malaysian history and an even more generous sweep of human emotions, universal and particular, specific to ethnic, gender and individual characters. I first met Edwin in Kuala Lumpur decades ago when he was composing his earliest poems. Going from strength to strength, this now prolific multi-genre writer and editor has emerged as an important literary figure in twenty-first century Malaysian Anglophone culture. The experiences narrated in his newest collection engage us with their pathos, learning, joy, and comic satire. *Have I Got Something to Tell You* is a welcomed contribution to our local and Southeast Asian literary wealth.'

—Shirley Geok-lin Lim, UCSB Professor Emerita,
poet, fictionist, memoirist and winner of
Commonwealth Poetry Prize and American
Books Awards

'Malachi Edwin Vethamini has something to say to us. His new anthology of short stories deals with the universal themes of love, loss, and cultural identity. At the same time, his stories are specifically rooted in the Indian, Malay, and Chinese cultures within the Malaysian social fabric. Particularly evocative are his stories around sibling love, gender-religious conflict, and a beautifully tender coming-of-age love triangle. Written from the heart, his stories remind us, as echoed by one of his characters, that it is okay to love too much.'

—Mahesh Dattani, playwright Sahitya
Akademi awardee, 1998

'The stories in this collection ripple with unsettling tensions. In the current political climate in Malaysia, friendship, love, kinship ties and family bonds are often complicated by race, religion, expectations, fears and prejudices against the Other. A very good read that offers the reader insights into Malaysia's vibrant minority Tamil community.'

—Suchen Christine Lim, novelist and short fiction writer, winner of Southeast Asia Write Award, Inaugural Singapore Literature Prize, and Singapore Cultural Medalion Award

Have I Got Something to Tell You

Stories by
Malachi Edwin Vethamani

PENGUIN BOOKS
An imprint of Penguin Random House

PENGUIN BOOKS

USA | Canada | UK | Ireland | Australia
New Zealand | India | South Africa | China | Southeast Asia

Penguin Books is part of the Penguin Random House group of companies
whose addresses can be found at global.penguinrandomhouse.com

Published by Penguin Random House SEA Pte Ltd
9, Changi South Street 3, Level 08-01,
Singapore 486361

First published in Penguin Books by Penguin Random House SEA 2024

10 9 8 7 6 5 4 3 2 1

This is a work of fiction. Names, characters, places and incidents
are either the product of the author's imagination or are used fictitiously,
and any resemblance to any actual person, living or dead, events or
locales is entirely coincidental. Some stories explore themes that are sensitive
and might not be suitable for some readers.

ISBN 9789815144857

Typeset in Garamond by MAP Systems, Bengaluru, India

www.penguin.sg

For my family:

Vincent, Julian, Ros, Amanie,
and
Aria Mikayla Julian Matthew Edwin

Contents

Rohan, Meg, and Lee

Two men stood grieving. Rohan stood next to Lee. They were facing a closed coffin. In it lay Meg, Lee's wife. She had died after a brief but painful battle against cancer. Meg suffered from the effects of the chemo. Lee suffered for Meg. And Rohan suffered for both—more for Lee, perhaps, on account of being his friend since childhood.

The crematorium staff indicated that it was time to say their final goodbyes. Lee nodded to them. The coffin was slowly drawn into the rectangular opening in the wall. Rohan saw Lee's body shudder. He placed his right arm on Lee's shoulder. Tears flowed down Lee's cheeks. Rohan gently squeezed his shoulder as he tried to hold back his own tears. His heart was breaking for Lee. Rohan heard again the words Lee had once uttered to him: 'You love too much.'

* * *

It's another Friday. The day starts with a double period of PE. Everyone is changing out of their uniforms and getting into

T-shirts and shorts. The transition is swift, accompanied by a little embarrassment, which is covered-up by some teasing and horseplay. They are rather uncomfortable looking at each other's near-naked bodies. Everyone's wearing underwear but there is still a modicum of discomfort. Shame is ingrained in their young minds.

Rohan was no sportsman. He was more a voyeur when it came to sports and boys. Lee was the main object of his voyeurism. From gangly primary school boys their bodies had filled out with the onset of puberty. This was more pronounced with Lee. Lee stood at six-foot-three. He had a full head of long straight hair—as long as the school rules permitted. He was one of the few teenage boys who did not have to worry about facial hair or sideburns. His arms and legs were pretty muscular, thanks to long hours on the volleyball and basketball courts. Rohan just barely reached Lee's shoulders. His head was covered by a mop of curly hair, trimmed short by regular visits to the family barber. Soon he would have to start shaving his facial hair as required by the school rules.

Playing court games during PE was made bearable for Rohan solely because of Lee. He was always chosen for Lee's team on account of being Lee's good friend, not for his playing skills. He wasn't the worst player in the team, but some of Lee's teammates would have been happy if Lee didn't always pick Rohan. There were some perks to being close friends with the captain of the team! Very early in their friendship Rohan discovered that Lee looked out for him. This drew Rohan closer to Lee.

They spent most afternoons at the school library. This became a regular thing during revision for their trial exams. They shared similar ambitions for higher education. However, their interests in sports were different, and so were their choice of subjects. Their financial backgrounds would see them going their separate ways after Sixth Form. But neither boy was looking that far ahead. They had to get over the immediate hurdle that was the Fifth Form.

When Rohan and Lee arrived at school, their school uniforms served the purpose of concealing signs of their economic differences. Studying hard and passing exams with flying colours was going to help them on their way to success in school. What awaited after that was less certain for Rohan. Over the years he had learned that Lee's father was a successful businessman. But nothing about Lee flaunted wealth. They ate almost the same food in the school canteen, and sometimes ate the lunch packed by Rohan's Amma. She would have clobbered him if she found out that he'd been sharing his egg sandwiches with a rich kid.

Over the years, their classmates had noticed their bond of friendship and occasionally teased them, 'You two like husband and wife. Always together.' The teasing, though sometimes repeated, never went very far. Neither boy was seen as sissy or *pondan*. They played sports and did well academically. It was said in jest, or when they wanted the two boys to work in different groups.

Then, the 13 May 1969 riots happened. Both were at their homes when the violence broke out and a nation-wide curfew was announced. Their homes were a distance away from the violence that was raging in city areas of Kuala Lumpur (KL). A period of enforced silence began between them. Rohan assumed that Lee was safe in his upper-middle-class family home in Petaling Jaya (PJ). Rohan's parents' flat in Brickfields—a neighbourhood known for its prominence amongst the Indian and Chinese in the community—felt safe.

As the violence was brought under control and there was some semblance of normality, Rohan found himself wanting to contact Lee. His friend's telephone number and address were neatly written in his little AIA pocket diary which his father had given him. A longing to hear Lee's voice emerged as his face appeared in his mind's eye.

Rohan took a few ten-sen coins and headed to the public phone booth. His mother did not like Rohan using the house phone. His Amma always feared that while he was on the line, she might miss an important call from his Periamma or her friends. He was hoping for a long, uninterrupted call with Lee. The phone had hardly begun ringing when a voice answered.

'Hello, Uncle, can I speak to Lee Kok Keong? I'm his classmate,' Rohan spoke to an elderly male voice on the other end, and assumed it was Lee's father. He heard Lee's named being called out, and a few Cantonese words followed.

'Hello,' a familiar voice came down the line.

'Hey! Rohan here.'

'Oh! Anything?'

'No, lah. Just wanted to say hi. How's your revision coming along?'

'Usual. Stupid Malays fighting and causing trouble.'

'Hope school will start again soon. Can study in the library again.'

'You not bothered by the fighting?'

'Just happy we are safe, lah.'

'Ha! Is that all you think of? You didn't hear about the changes that will be coming in this country? They will affect us, the non-Malays.'

Rohan was not prepared for this conversation. They had not spoken much about Malaysian politics before. It was always schoolwork stuff. *Where did this new person come from,* Rohan wondered.

'I heard some things. My father was talking to my uncles. I didn't pay much attention. More worried about my mathematics and general science, lah.'

'Better think about your future in this country. The future is not so good for us.'

'Really? I hope not. We have nowhere else to go. Your father said anything about migrating?'

'No, lah. He just asked me to study hard so I can go overseas for my university studies.'

Rohan's heart sank on hearing about university studies. He wasn't sure why. He had always known that Lee would probably go overseas after Sixth Form. It wouldn't be easy for a Chinese boy to get into the Medical Faculty in University of Malaya. He didn't want to think of what might happen after Sixth Form.

* * *

He had been friends with Lee from the time they started primary school. A few of his friends had been in the same class right up to Fifth Form. Separation was inevitable after this year, he knew. Many would not go on to Sixth Form. There was talk of working or pursuing a diploma. Rohan would have to do well to get into Sixth Form in a government school. He saw no other way to continue his studies. And after that, only local universities were his options.

Their conversation did not last much longer. There was someone standing rather close to Rohan, waiting for his turn to use the phone.

'There's someone waiting to use the phone.'

'Let them wait, lah.'

'No, lah. I'll call again soon.'

'I'll call you on your house phone one of these days.'

Lee never called Rohan on his house phone. It was his way of saying goodbye on the phone. That was how it had been over the years and Rohan was used to it.

* * *

School did eventually re-open. Everyone went back to class as if nothing had happened. It was only much later that they heard about school mates whose homes had been burned down in the Chow Kit area. Fortunately, they all managed to escape with their lives.

The Fifth Form examination loomed heavily upon them. In a few months, that too would no longer be a concern. What to do while waiting for the results would then become the main concern. Neither Rohan nor Lee had family-businesses to work in.

Walking along Petaling Street and going to the Rex Cinema became a regular thing. On Saturdays Lee accompanied his father to his office. Rohan and Lee would meet around 10 a.m. and go on to do what they had planned over the phone. There were record shops that sold cheap pirated records they could afford, and there was no limit to the number of food stalls they could frequent. They fell into an easy companionship and were quite oblivious to others around them. Once, as they were sharing an apple, Rohan saw a young child looking aghast as Lee took a bite of an apple Rohan had just bitten into. It was too shocking for him to see a Chinese and an

Indian boy share an apple. The mixing of racial saliva was too much to watch.

They often caught the Saturday midday matinees. The cheapest eighty-five-sen ticket was affordable. As the lights went down, Rohan would put his head on Lee's shoulder. Lee did not move away. It had begun as an accident and then it just continued. The smell of Lee's hair cream wafted towards Rohan, and he inhaled both, the smell of the sweat from Lee's neck and the hair cream.

Bored with nothing much to do during the three-month wait for their results, Rohan and Lee signed up for a character-building camp in Cameron Highlands. Their parents thought it was a good idea. For Rohan it meant that for the first time he would be spending three whole days with Lee. They shared a room with two other boys. There were two big beds for the four of them. The first night was rather cold, and they drew close to each other to keep warm. Rohan was once again confronted with the familiar smell of Lee's hair cream. The next night Rohan moved closer to Lee. Lee turned and faced Rohan. There was a brushing of lips. And their hands moved to grope each other. It was frantic and fast. Both felt a wetness in their pyjamas. Rohan kissed Lee again and Lee responded. He then uttered, 'You love too much,' and fell asleep. Lee's words continued to ring in Rohan's head, and he, too, eventually fell asleep.

A mere tumbling in the bed it was not, for Rohan. The brushing of lips and then the reciprocated kiss were stamped into Rohan's being, and it bound Lee to Rohan like Gatsby to Daisy upon their first kiss. And like Daisy, unbeknownst to Rohan, Lee would be beyond Rohan's grasp, never to be his beloved.

In the morning, they rose and got ready for breakfast and the first workshop session of the day. Lee looked at Rohan no differently than the day before. It was as if nothing had happened the previous night. Later, after lunch, they set out on a hike. Rohan walking close to Lee, asked, 'What did you mean by "I love too much"?'

'Ya, lah. That's what I meant. You love too much. No need to overthink what I said.' Lee moved on slightly ahead of Rohan, ending the conversation.

Rohan looked at Lee, puzzled. They had not talked of love, but Lee had used the l-word again. He wasn't really sure what Lee meant by love. He certainly felt a strong affection for Lee. And the previous night they had kissed, and even done more than kissing. At the emotional level it had not fully registered for him. Did Lee love him? Or was it that Rohan loved Lee too much? These questions rang out loud in Rohan's mind. The events of the day kept them both busy with the other participants. That night, worn out by a long hike, they both fell asleep as soon as their heads hit the pillow.

What happened in Cameron Highlands remained in Cameron Highlands. It was as if the sexual intimacy had never happened, and Lee had not said the four words Rohan heard that night and again the next morning. They returned home, and when the Fifth Form results were announced, they returned to school and continued to be in the same class. Towards the latter part of the second year of Sixth Form it became clear that Lee was going to go abroad. He started applying for medical colleges in England and Ireland. Rohan did not hunger for Lee in any sexual way. There was physical closeness, but never a hug, let alone a kiss. There was the usual rubbing of shoulders and pressing of calves. Their strong bond of friendship deepened.

They both did well in their exams. Lee had straight A's but didn't get an offer to study medicine at the University of Malaya. Rohan scored two A's and two B's, and had not bothered to apply for medicine or any science programmes. Lee was offered a place at the School of Medical Sciences at the University of Manchester. Rohan was quite happy getting admission to do a mass communications degree in Universiti Sains Malaysia in Penang. He decided that he would take up a career in journalism or advertising. He was fulfilling his parents' dream of having a son with a university qualification. Rohan also wanted to move away from KL. There were too many memories of Lee here, and he knew he was bound to feel lonely.

Just before Rohan started his university studies, Lee suggested a two-night holiday in Port Dickson. They took a bus from KL to Seremban and then another to Port Dickson. They found a cheap two-storey hotel near a public beach. It was a bit rough, with no attached bath and toilet facilities. At least there was air-conditioning and a clean big bed. They lay in bed reading, waiting for cooler temperatures. They were in their shorts, the outfit reminiscent of their time in school, and more specifically, of the time they spent in PE class. The bed was big, with enough space to move around. Rohan had his head on Lee's shoulder.

The sun was beginning to sneak away. They headed to the beach. Neither could swim and so they remained standing shoulder deep in the water. After some splashing about they sat on the beach, their feet digging into the sand.

'Do you think you might come and visit me?' Lee asked.

'You paying for the holiday?'

'Yeah, right! I'll just ask my father to pay for my buddy to visit me. I'm sure he'll oblige.'

Rohan looked at Lee. 'I'm your buddy, that I am.' The talk of separation began to gnaw into Rohan. He wanted to hold Lee and kiss him hard on the mouth. He wanted to hear Lee say, 'You love too much' again. However, no mention of the L-word was made. It might hint to Rohan that Lee loved him too. *This hot weather is not going to help my cause,* he thought to himself. So here we are. I want to hear him say, 'you love too much'.

The rest of the day went by uneventfully. Despite the walks and dips in the sea, neither boy was hungry. After a light dinner, they got into bed. Lee switched off the lights and Rohan moved towards Lee and hugged him. By this time Rohan was already sobbing. Lee turned and hugged him back. He felt Rohan's hot tears on his chest. They held each other. Rohan slowly regained his composure as he calmed down.

'I'm going to miss you miserably.'

A silence.

'I've become so accustomed to your voice. We talk on the phone when we aren't together.' That they had done. Rohan was a regular feature at the public pay phone on weekends and long holiday breaks.

Silence.

'Lee, will you miss me?'

'Of course, lah. Why all these tears? We knew this would happen. You have known my plans all along.'

Rohan breathed deep, remembering the familiar scent of the young man next to him. Lee hugged Rohan. 'I told you before, you love too much. I love you, lah. Rohan don't think too much. The next few years will go by quickly. And then we will both be in KL again. We will have money and we can travel and see the world.'

Rohan sighed. He felt Lee's arms around him. Lee was silent. Slowly Lee disentangled himself from Rohan. He turned around and soon Rohan heard a light snoring. He too turned his back to Lee. His left hand slipped into his shorts, and he remembered their night in Cameron Highlands.

* * *

The next few years were equally busy for both the boys. The close proximity they had shared over many years was now replaced by cheap aerogramme communication, occasional greeting cards and mailed photographs. Lee replied to Rohan's letters and surprised Rohan with yearly birthday gifts. This was new development, and it pleased Rohan. This euphoria was replaced with some unsettling thoughts when Rohan received a photograph of Lee in his bathrobe, holding a toothbrush and standing in-front of a mirror. The delight at seeing Lee's face quickly disappeared as Rohan wondered who had taken the photo and spent the night with him. It did not strike him then that the photographer could be a woman.

Staying away from home and living among new acquaintances gave Rohan a new sense of freedom. The pang of jealousy that Rohan had felt looking at Lee was soon replaced with guilt. He rationalized to himself that he thought Lee was sleeping around because that was what he found himself was doing. Sex was an urge and desire. Once the act was over, the person meant nothing to him. Lee remained for him the one he loved. He had hoped for some sexual intimacy but that had passed. He wanted a loving relationship. He would settle for the love of bosom friends, like that shared by David and Jonathan many centuries ago. Rohan wanted a love that was mutual and constant. A friendship that would give them both happiness. He would settle for that love without sex. When Lee had said that Rohan 'loved too much' Rohan didn't agree with him. How could anyone love too much? Lee had said he loved Rohan. That was enough. This was the happiness he wanted.

For Rohan their love was a passionate friendship which had once slipped to sexual intimacy. Rohan no longer ached with desire for Lee. This primal desire could be gratified with the anonymous and attractive men he encountered on campus and in the city. Rohan's sexual encounters had nothing to do with happiness. It was not love. It was sex, necessary, and other men could satisfy this need, if Lee would not.

* * *

The university years passed quickly, as Lee had said they would. Now, the cocoon of campus life was broken. Rohan found himself with a job as a writer for a men's magazine. He remained in Penang. There was no lack of good, cheap food in Penang, and he could live quite comfortably. His family was a safe distance away. He found an affordable apartment near his workplace. His job gave him opportunities for a social life and meeting men.

He discovered the gym during his varsity days. He wasn't interested in building muscles but he certainly wanted a well-toned body. Just as he looked at a person first before he decided on his next move, he felt he was judged the same way. He kept his three-day training routine as regularly as possible. At the gym in the university, he had abided by his rule to keep it strictly about workouts and not looking at other male bodies. Later, when he joined another gym, he kept very much to himself. It was after all a gym and not a cruising ground. He rarely initiated a conversation, but should an attractive man start a conversation he would respond, and within a few exchanges he could tell where the conversation was going. He was not loudly open about his sexuality but he did not hide it either.

With his salary, he could now afford short international calls. Rohan and Lee had to work out the best time for when the rates were the cheapest and both were awake and not at work or university. It felt like their school-day weekend phone calls. The only difference was that Rohan was not standing in a public phone booth and there was no one standing behind him.

During one of these phone calls, the inevitable was mentioned. Lee told Rohan that he has been seeing a Malaysian-Chinese girl. It was quite clear that it was more than just seeing. So, it was no surprise when a few months later he mentioned her name and said he was going to get engaged to Meg.

'My parents approve of her,' Lee said.

'I'm happy for you. For you both,' Rohan responded.

Rohan felt no anger or hurt. He believed Lee's love for him remained unchanged. He was not losing Lee to another man. But all the talk of travelling together suddenly vanished, and he felt an emptiness, a feeling of loss.

* * *

Rohan had enough savings to make the trip to London to be Lee's best man. Rohan met Meg the day he arrived at London. Meg and Lee were sharing a one-room apartment and Rohan slept in the pull-out sofa bed in the hall for the few days that he was there. She was pleasant, and he could see why Lee had fallen for her.

They went to London Chinatown for a Chinese meal. Meg, Rohan and Lee sat at a small round table that was just right for three people. You could not tell who was sitting between whom. Meg and Lee looked the happy couple about to take their marriage vows with Rohan playing the best man for the groom.

The wedding ceremony was simple—taking the vows and signing the registry before the registrar of marriages in a government office. There were about twenty people in the wedding party. Rohan knew they were mostly family members and he was probably the only outsider, the only Indian, present. A wedding banquet would be held in Kuala Lumpur for more family members and friends when the couple returned to Malaysia in the summer.

Rohan did a few touristy things in London, caught a West-End musical, visited the Covent Garden Market, went to Madame Tussaud's and watched the Changing of the Guard at Whitehall. He could not pluck up enough courage to go to a gay bar, let alone to a gay sauna. He did not get to spend any time alone with Lee either. Rohan was ready to return home. He would now have to get used to there being three of them—Lee, Meg, and him.

Lee and Meg returned to Kuala Lumpur a few months later, as planned. They had the wedding banquet at a well-known Chinese restaurant, chosen by Lee's father, the restaurant owner being his father's friend. Rohan played the best man role again. This time he got drunk as the evening drew on. His drunkenness was quite obvious as he was no longer able to accompany the couple to the different tables to meet and toast the newlyweds. Rohan held on to one of his friends and then broke down. He cried. It might not have been obvious to the others, but Lee saw Rohan from a distance. He asked one of their mutual friends to discreetly take him back to the hotel.

* * *

'Is Rohan more than your best friend? Is he in love with you?' Meg asked.

Lee was taken aback by Meg's direct questioning. She had actually mentioned the word 'love'. Lee turned and looked at his wife. He wanted to assure her that she had nothing to fear. He replied in all honesty to his wife.

'Rohan is my best friend. He was in love with me. I care a lot for him, and I love him as a very dear friend. But I do not love him the way I love you.

'He's my soulmate. We've known each other all our lives. We've looked out for each other. Shared growing pains. I'd lie if I said that I didn't love him but my friendship with Rohan is not a threat to us.

'I really want you know that he's never been a threat to us. He wouldn't want to hurt you or me or us. That's Rohan. It might be hard for you to understand. He's no interloper and I'm proud of my love for him. We saw each other through our school and undergrad days.'

Meg listened. She watched her husband speak with all earnestness about Rohan. She did not know enough about

Rohan but Lee's love for her was genuine, and Lee had no sexual attraction towards Rohan.

'But does Rohan love you now the same way as you care for him?'

'Yes. He has come to understand the way I love him and feel for him. He accepts it. That it is the only way we can be friends.'

'Is that why Rohan got drunk and cried at our wedding banquet? The thought that he was losing you must have finally sunk in.

'*Keong*, he is gay. I can tell. I never sensed any antagonism towards me from the day he came to stay at our home in London. I think he even likes me.'

'He does, Meg.'

Meg looked at her husband. She knew Lee loved her. She had sensed a closeness between these two men. She trusted her husband and she felt a sense of relief.

Meg never spoke of Rohan's relationship with Lee again. Lee was so relieved that they had spoken about Rohan. He was relieved that Meg knew how he cared for this man who had loved him from his school days. He was relieved that he did not have to lie about Rohan, and Meg did not have to feel that there was a third person in their marriage.

* * *

Rohan returned to Penang after the wedding banquet and made no plans to return to Kuala Lumpur for work. His life in Penang had taken on a certain familiarity and his work routine appealed to him. He worked eight-to-five and then played. He was also far from family and family friends.

Returning to Kuala Lumpur was an annual event, a trip made so he could spend Deepavali with his family. It was usually a short stay at the family home with his parents and two younger sisters. He did not meet the guests who visited his parents. He remained in his childhood room—now turned guest room—in the family house. He felt a bit of a stranger, among his own family, having been away for so long. During these annual trips, just as he was beginning to get comfortable it was time to leave. He knew, if he stayed any longer, his mother would start asking about his future plans, and that meant talking about marriage.

* * *

One evening was set aside for dinner with Lee and Meg during Rohan's annual Deepavali visits to KL. They met at the Selangor Club. Lee's dad had transferred his membership to his son. Lee used it for his gym, and to host dinners with contacts from his professional network.

'You both should come visit me in Penang, we can have a meal by the sea at the Penang Club. I finally got my membership.'

'Someone's doing very well for himself to get a membership at that exclusive club,' Lee teased Rohan.

'Hey! Now I can even buy you a meal here, at your club,' Rohan replied.

'Let's not change things the way it's been for us,' Lee said.

That's how it's been for us, Rohan thought to himself. Very convenient for this relationship. He looked at Meg and couldn't help but feel a tinge of envy. He couldn't resent her. It was Lee who had determined the course of their relationship, and Rohan had chosen to stay in it, and not lose his friend.

Meg looked slightly pale and moved in a deliberately slower manner. Rohan made no comment. That was the last time the three of them had their annual Deepavali dinner together. Lee and Meg did not take up his invitation to come to Penang.

It was only a few months later that Lee told Rohan over the phone that Meg had been diagnosed with leukaemia. They tried to keep in touch. They were both in the same time zone but it was becoming more and more difficult, especially for Lee. Rohan would call late evenings, and if Lee did not pick up the phone, he took it that Lee was busy. Lee would return his calls and they would talk about Meg, and how Lee was coping. The calls were often brief, but it was the only way for the two men to maintain close contact.

Over the next three years Meg waged an impressive battle against the monster that was cancer. Rohan heard about her struggle and sensed the pain it caused Lee. Lee and Meg returned to London for treatment. Lee did all he could for Meg. They could afford the best medical care but even that was not enough to save his wife. He brought her home to Kuala Lumpur to be with their families. Rohan did not get to say goodbye to Meg. He heard of her passing over the phone from a sobbing Lee.

Rohan was the first person he called.

Perhaps it was all right to love too much.

In Close Proximity

When Bala recalled May 13, 1969, it was not the violence that usually sprang to his mind; it was the memory of eating cream crackers with butter. He could still feel the first taste on his tongue, the crumbling of the crackers and the smooth butter against his palate. Its slightly salty taste remained stamped in his memory.

Uncle Param had brought bags of food for his family when the curfew had been lifted for a few hours. Bala had never eaten cream crackers with butter, it had always been with margarine. But his father's friend had bought loads of groceries for them, including two whole slabs of butter! Bala had not realized there would be such a difference in the taste. He would painstakingly cut thin slices of frozen butter from the small slab and place them delicately on the crackers. He was more than willing to patiently cut these slices than settle for the easy spread of margarine to which he was accustomed.

The fears that were real to Bala during the first few days of the riots had not been about the violence. Thoughts of being harmed or killed did not loom in his head. His kampong felt quite safe. He had more immediate concerns. The curfew was one major source of worry. It had made going to the toilet against the law and the family latrine was situated at least fifty metres from their back door. His father's matter-of-fact approach to this problem was of no help to him. Bala didn't fancy getting shot at by the army. To make matters worse, Jaya, his elder brother teased him, 'Soldiers don't shoot boys in towels going to shit.'

Bala did all he could to control himself, and only went out when he could no longer bear it. Once in the toilet, he worried about making his return dash back to the house. This situation went on for a few days, and his anxiety never lessened. Getting shot at while wearing just his towel was certainly distasteful but the thought of getting killed in it was utterly unbearable.

On one of his excursions to the toilet, Bala looked at the bucket below him and saw that it was already half full. The night-soil removers had not been coming to empty the buckets. He was horror-struck. *If they don't come in the next couple of days, what are we going to do?* He wondered. The new problem now tormented him more than his fear of breaking the curfew or getting shot. This he could not discuss with anyone.

He kept his fears to himself. It was something the family had never talked about. Toilet buckets got emptied every night by an invisible force. It was a fact of life which did not require comment and now he did not know how he could broach the subject. *Things like these are supposed to take care of themselves*, he thought. In his heart, he did not want to know what might have to be done if the men did not come at night. He hoped things would get sorted out, somehow.

The stench if it overflowed . . . he half-thought and stopped, unable to go on.

* * *

Bala looked at the textbook in front of him. Jaya had told him that school would resume soon and his school examination would not be postponed. He had been warned that he would have to study on his own as his teachers might not be able to complete the syllabus.

'*Annan*, what'll happen if my school is burnt down?' he asked.

'Shut up and study,' Jaya replied. This had become his standard reply for most of Bala's questions.

'Annan, why are the people fighting?' Bala asked, hoping to get a break from geography.

'You wouldn't understand. Just read your book. Anyway, it doesn't really concern us. It's between the Malays and Chinese.'

'But . . .'

'Shut up and study,' Jaya cut in sharply before Bala could ask another question.

'Between the Malays and Chinese,' Bala thought and remembered his friends at school. There were very few Malay students at his school. Zainal was the only Malay boy in his class and Zainal usually kept to himself during class and joined his Malay friends from the other classes during the break. Most of the Chinese boys also kept to themselves. Bala could not understand why people should be fighting and killing each other.

Bala looked down at his book and continued reading about the rubber industry in Malaysia. Lots of Indians in the rubber estates, he knew. He was glad he was not living there. He had a few classmates from a nearby rubber estate. They spoke little English and they, too, kept to themselves. His other classmates often teased them for being dirty and stinky. Bala felt sorry for them but never spoke up in their defence. In his class, Bala sat next to a Chinese boy. Bala did not quite belong to any group and did not want to, either.

Fear flashed through him as he remembered Siew Heng. He wondered if Siew Heng was all right. Siew Heng's father was a successful shopkeeper. A driver brought Siew Heng to school every morning. In the afternoons, Bala and Siew Heng would walk along Petaling Street to Siew Heng's father's shop and Bala would walk on to the bus-stop and return home. That was all he knew of Siew Heng.

Bala was still reading his geography book when Uncle Param arrived. This time, he was not carrying any plastic bags of goodies as he usually did. He didn't look his usual bright self, either. He spoke in hushed tones with Bala's father. Bala couldn't hear their conversation, but he knew something was wrong.

Jaya joined the other men. Jaya stood listening, saying nothing. His face also turned grim. Bala's father began to shake his head. Uncle Param touched his father's shoulders. Bala wanted to join the adults but did not dare. He wanted to know what they were saying, but looking at his father's face, he thought better of it. His uneasiness grew. Then his mother joined in the conversation and soon after she started crying.

* * *

The next few years drew on rather uneventfully for Bala. Going to college, a teacher's training college at that, slowly began to loosen family ties. He dreaded the early years of teaching in a primary school. Minding other people's young children was not a long-term plan. Things, he felt, were finally going his way when he managed to get a Full Certificate for his Sixth Form examination. He sent his results with his application to be placed on a higher salary grade. Fortunately, his application was successful. He got more that he had anticipated. He was transferred to a secondary school in another town. *No more students running around my knees,* he thought to himself.

Bala arrived in Banting with no second thoughts about his move. He had often wanted to find a place of his own. The new job was a good enough reason for his leaving home. Although it was slightly more than an hour from his parents' home, the roads after Klang were poor and winding. Everyone agreed that he should find a place of his own in Banting.

Banting was a small town, a far cry from what was happening in Kuala Lumpur and PJ. But Bala was glad to be away from KL. The city had become rife with political uncertainty. This was unprecedented. Bala was used to the ongoing protests from the opposition parties and with leadership struggles in the Chinese and Indian political parties. They never seemed to threaten any real national repercussions.

For the first time, there was major conflict among the Malay leaders in government. This brought fear, as he knew well that any open conflict could only result in instability and trouble for all. He knew that any trouble among the Malays could lead to problems with other communities. The school staff room was quite representative of the nation.

The small number of Indian and Chinese teachers stayed out of the political discussions. Still, you could tell who the opposition party supporters were. The Malay teachers who were women were less vocal while the Malay men seemed to thrive on political debate, which often bordered on argument when opposing party members got involved. Tension simmered beneath the veneer of outward civility.

May 13, 1969, might have been eighteen years ago. Today, it was not the butter and cream crackers Bala remembered but the death of his cousin and the deaths of many, many others. He did not want the Malay government's leadership trouble to lead to any violence. Being in Banting kept him away from all rumours and speculations. The less he knew, the better he felt.

Bala was relieved when the Prime Minister's team finally emerged victorious, although the party was split. He did not worry too much as he placed great faith in the Prime Minister's political shrewdness and survival instinct. The affairs of state began to settle again, unlike Bala's own, which moved in unexpected directions. He met a Malay girl at a party and unlike the other women he was used to, she was rather disconcerting.

Bala was now treading uncharted territory. In early childhood, his father had cautioned all his children: marry your own kind. Chinese people eat pork and will call you a bastard when they're angry. And for Malays, don't even think about it. You will lose your name and family. But here he was with Rashidah on his mind, constantly. Bala wanted his private life to be his own and keep his father and matters of race and religion, out of it, and firmly in the public space. *The two don't need to meet or collide*, he thought to himself.

* * *

Bala had lain on his hospital bed, his right arm in a cast. His whole body ached, his head and the whole of his right side hurt even more. He had been postponing pressing the bell for a bedpan. Before he could make up his mind, he dozed off . . .

I am being led to some of the guests in the party by Raman. An attractive woman in the group catches my attention. I shake hands with the guests. At the mention of her name, I place her. Rashidah had caught my attention a few days ago at an in-service teacher training course and I am pleased to meet her again. The conversation quickly slips into innuendo. Rashidah deflates Raman's boast of sexual prowess with a line on how women have perfected the art of faking orgasms. Rashidah speaks excellent English and has a great sense of humour. When I compliment her, she boasts, 'Hey, I'm a convent girl, you know! We should be all right with the missionary position, then.' I teasingly tell her I went to an Anglican secondary school. 'I've furthered my education since then, actually,' she replies.

Bala was glad that his family had been unable to get him a first-class hospital room. He did not want to be alone. He was also happy with the restricted visiting hours. He waited for the eight o'clock hospital bell. He wanted his mother to leave. Her presence was a constant reminder of the pain he had inflicted on her. She also kept reminding him periodically of his apparent lack of concern for his family's feelings.

He rang the bell for the nurse and when she came, he told her that he was in pain and wanted another *Ponstan* capsule. She told Bala that he was not due for one for the next two hours. 'I'll ask Sister if I can give you the medicine now,' she told him. He hoped the Sister would give in to his request.

'Amma, you better go now. I want to take the medicine. It will help me sleep for a while.'

His mother nodded and began to gather the tiffin carrier and her thermos flask. 'What do you want to eat tomorrow, Bala?' she asked in Tamil.

'Anything, Amma. Don't trouble yourself, please,' he sincerely urged her. 'Hospital food is okay,' he lied. The cream crackers his mother had brought lay uneaten. Looking at them now he hated them and the taste of butter melting in his mouth was lost to him. 'Please take the biscuits back with you; I don't want them, Amma.'

His mother placed her hand on Bala's and bade him farewell. The nurse returned with his medicine. He accepted it gratefully and soon began to sleep . . .

Rashidah nudges me gently as I pretend to sleep. She kisses me on my lips. The smile that breaks across my face ruins my game of pretend. I slip my fingers between her legs. She is still wet. I move on top of her and enter her. 'Hey, missionary, we've got other things to do,' she protests weakly. 'What's so urgent?' I ask, not losing my rhythm, half remembering what we had earlier planned. 'My brother's expecting us for lunch,' Rashidah reminds me. I stop. Rashidah now says we are in no hurry. I roll off her and look into her eyes. She looks perturbed. 'You did agree, you know.' She tries to make it sound as though she is coaxing me. 'Yeah, I know. Just getting cold feet.' 'Well, that's not all. You got me started and just stopped. Thank you very much!' I apologize. 'Meeting my prospective in-laws is a major event, you know!' Rashidah is silent. 'He's not going to ask if I have started the conversion procedures, is he?' I ask in a near whisper. 'I think he will,' she replies, with a straight face. I look at her again, unsure if she is serious. 'What have you told him about us?' I query. 'I told him you're great in bed and the myths about Indian men are true.' She laughs. 'What did you think I told him?' She now asks me. 'I don't know. I guess I'm just nervous.

Tell me what to expect,' I plead. 'You know I love you. We just need to take this slowly. I've yet to break the news to my side,' I reassure her.

* * *

The last five days had been quite unbearable. Bala was pleased that he had finally been allowed to get out of his bed. *No more bedpans*, Bala thought to himself. He had enjoyed the warm shower and had only just emerged when the nurse came to complain that he had been there too long.

Bala's body had ached less but he continued to have sharp pains in the back of his head. The pain remained dull most of the time, but occasionally, he would feel stabbing pains. He moved in his bed, trying to find a comfortable position. He was due for another painkiller. He knew that it would help him fall asleep . . .

'Come join me for roti canai,' Wahab, the Chemistry teacher invites me. 'How's Hasnah?' I inquire. 'OK. The baby's due in two weeks,' he replies in a rather distracted fashion. 'I heard they are going to raid your flat tonight,' Wahab blurts a warning. 'I heard the Ustaz saying that the Jabatan Ugama has received some complaints about you committing khalwat. Be careful not to have your-er-girlfriend over tonight.' 'What else do you know?' I ask. 'That's all. Any way, I don't have to tell you what they'll do to you both if you're caught,' Wahab warns. I move uncomfortably in my chair.

* * *

Bala had lain miserable in bed. His family and his old friend, Raman, had been his only visitors. The person he wanted most had not come. Raman conveyed Rashidah's concern for Bala's health and that was all he ever said. Bala could not bring himself to ask if she sent her love. Not because that would embarrass Raman, but because he feared Rashidah might have said nothing of it. His thoughts kept slipping into the past and often he could not make out if he were asleep, awake or just dreaming. Daydreams, dreams, and nightmares collided constantly . . .

'Assalamualaikum,' Rashidah greets Karim as she enters his house.' Malaikumuassalum,' two voices reply. 'Shidah tells us that you got your Proton only last week,' Karim begins. 'Yeah, driving it is so much better than riding my bike,' I reply. 'Shidah has told us a lot about you. We're happy to meet you finally,' Karim goes on. 'Me too. She's often spoken about you, too.' Rashidah is speaking to her sister-in-law in Malay. Rashidah turns to Karim and starts another conversation in Malay. Karim draws me into the conversation asking how's my work. 'Abang, thanks for lunch,' Rashidah is speaking in Malay. Shaking Karim's hand, I add, 'Thanks for having us.' 'It's been nice meeting you. Do come again,' Karim says as we get into the car. 'Now, that wasn't too difficult, was it?' Rashidah jests. 'No, actually it was quite pleasant,' I reply.' Please come in for some tea,' Rashidah coaxes me when we arrive at her place. I remain seated in the hall at her flat. Rashidah returns with a plate of biscuits. She sits next to me and places one in my mouth. The door suddenly flings open. A few masked men rush into the room. One of them shouts 'Sundal' at Rashidah. We are too shocked to do anything. Before we could react, two men rush at Rashidah and pull her away. The blows on my head and body then begin. I attempt to protect my head with my hands and expose my body to their blows. All I hear is Rashidah screaming. It grows dark and silent.

* * *

Bala's family had been informed of the attack. When his parents and brother arrived at the hospital, Rashidah was by his side. He had regained consciousness but now lay in a sedated asleep. Rashidah said nothing. Bala's mother held her son's hand and wept quietly. His father stood silently by his wife. Rashidah bade farewell and left.

The police had returned the following morning for Bala's description of his assailants. He gave none. He thought it was all a farce. He knew the police were aware of the nature of his case but never broached the issue.

The whole affair made him sick.

Shitting in the bed pan. Eating cream crackers but still hungering for Rashidah.

The Kiss

When Periappa died a few minutes before midnight, Periamma stood by his hospital bed crying quietly. My mother stood next to her sister, her eyes watering, but she didn't say a word. They had constantly been by his side for the last two weeks, taking care of him until the very end.

Poor Periamma, I thought. I had seen her in tears so many, many times. Periappa, now lying on the bed, very dead, had been the cause of much of her sorrow and pain. Yet,there she was, crying. I knew she was crying for him, her husband. Even if he had been her husband and even if he had hit her many, many times. She still wanted him alive.

Seeing her, I wanted to cry, too. But just for her. Periamma loved me dearly. Pati used to say that when Periamma held me as a baby, she used to coo endearments at me in exhilaration. I wanted to cry. Still, my tears never came.

My cousins went about making arrangements to take their dead father back home. Except for my eldest cousin who was still crying, all the others were dry-eyed. I was relieved that it was all finally over. Periappa had been at the hospital many times before. We had not expected him to pull through this time. I had secretly wished he would not die in the middle of my MCE examinations. That would have upset me.

My exams were over now, and my uncle could very well die, and I would give him all the time his death demanded of me. It is not that I did not like Periappa. He was a likeable sort of person, in his own way. I do have fond memories of him. It is just that when I begin to get nostalgic and sentimental about him, the unpleasant things about him started creeping up in my thoughts.

'Appa's back from work. You want to go for drive or not?' Malar, one of my cousins, would ask.

The expressions on my face, my younger brother's and my other cousin's gave the expected reply. We scampered into the old Holden. There weren't too many people with cars at that time. Periappa was among the three or four in our kampung who did. BA600 was the car number plate. Often, when we saw those magical numbers returning home, it meant we were in for a drive. But only if Periappa was in a good mood, and that unfortunately usually meant, a drinking mood.

All of us knew the route Periappa would take and his destination. We also knew what was expected of us throughout the drive. There used to be at least four of us in his car, my cousin-sisters who were both around my age, my younger brother, and me.

As we got into the car, he would usually ask my brother and me, 'Dei, your mother knows you're going for a drive with Periappa?' And we always lied that she did. We had been warned many, many times not to go with Periappa when he offered us a drive, especially if Periamma was not in the car. We ignored our mother's warning. The fear of being scolded by Amma was nothing compared to the excitement of going for a drive in Periappa's car.

Getting into the back seat of the car, we would fight for window seats. It was usually me and Malar who got them; the other two being younger, usually lost out. We did allow them the privilege once in a while, after much begging and bargaining on their part, of course.

Taking Periappa's body three floors up a narrow flight of stairs was a tricky business. I imagined his knees buckling as the coffin-bearers tilted it upwards, forgetting that rigor mortis must have set in.

As they brought the coffin into the small hall, the women wailed loudly. I decided to stay outside. A knot began to tighten in my stomach. The wailing and weeping continued for what seemed like a long time. Just as it was about to subside, another female friend or relative would turn up to pay her respects and there would be a new wave of loud weeping. More than anything else, I wanted to throw up.

Most of these people did not like Periappa, despite their sudden show of sorrow. It was a show and it disgusted me. Looking at Periamma, I felt sorry for her. She had suffered much with Periappa. Now she had to put up with these people and their pretence. Periappa was not the most popular person in our kampung.

Periamma had been given a chair and she was seated next to Periappa's coffin by his head. Periappa lay dressed in a white, long-sleeved shirt and a well-ironed vest. His hands were folded just below his chest. His hair was neatly combed, and he did have a pleasant look on his face, despite all the pain he had been through before his eventual death.

'Pastor's coming, Pastor's coming,' my cousins started announcing. As the pastor came in, Periamma got up to greet him. He moved towards her and touched her gently on her shoulders and said something to her. He asked her to sit down. Periamma did. He flashed a cursory smile at the others that were present. I avoided eye contact with him.

Hymn books appeared from nowhere and soon almost everyone had one each. My cousin who was helping distribute the books did not bother to give me one. Soon page numbers were being suggested and Tamil hymns were being sung solemnly and this was better than listening to the weeping.

Periappa used to have a powerful singing voice. When he attended church services, which was not often, his loud voice could be heard when Tamil hymns were sung. Most choir members could not read Tamil. They held the hymn books in front of them and pretended to sing. He outdid them handsomely.

Periappa did not take us on drives on Sundays. He, too seemed, to have observed the Sabbath, in his own way. Our drives were usually after his work. Periappa used to sell cloth and sewing materials. He would drive off to estates that were far away from our kampung in Sentul. There, opening his car-boot, he would sell to Indians who could not afford to pay him in cash. He had a book where he kept his accounts, organized according to families.

The Pastor was saying a prayer and heads were thus bowed. Just as I was about to do the same, someone touched me on my shoulder. It was Athan, my brother-in-law. I had not seen him since his arrival from Seremban. I walked out of the hall, and we went downstairs.

'Heard you were a brave boy and gave blood,' he said, in what sounded like an attempt at misplaced humour.

'Periappa was losing quite a lot of blood and the doctors wanted donors, so I volunteered,' I replied, thinking it was a small repayment for all those joy rides in his car.

Periappa mattered little to Athan. He hardly knew him, Athan having been only recently married to my sister. Athan was not into hymns and prayers, either. We went downstairs and walked towards the funeral tent.

Appa was seated among the men who had come pay their respects to Periappa. He looked tired. Appa did not have a car, just a bicycle. Appa was also not like Periappa. Appa was all work, no drinks at all. He did not take us anywhere, either. He wanted us to study hard and go to university. Periappa let my cousins do whatever they wanted. I had envied them endlessly.

Athan sat next to Appa and I reluctantly moved to join my father. The next thing I knew, we had been given funeral duties. Appa told us that we were to look after the wreaths that were being brought. Immediately I regretted coming down. I decided I would pass the buck to the first male cousin I saw. He was their father, after all. Not mine.

* * *

Periappa's car was parked near the tent. It now seemed old and rickety. It had always been old and rickety, but that had not mattered to us. Periappa behind the wheel was a different man. After asking if we had got our mother's permission to go out with him, he would drive in silence, unusually quiet. It was like we were almost invisible to him.

He would drive slowly towards the toddy shop in Jalan San Peng. The drive there lasted about twenty minutes, but it had seemed much longer. We were not walking, and we were the envy of our friends whom we passed along the way. Arriving at the toddy shop, Periappa would instruct us to wind up our windows and lock the doors. We did. We knew what would happen next.

Periappa would buy *kacang putih* and *vadai* and bring them to us. Unlocking the door, we would gratefully accept them and start sharing the food equally among ourselves. As we busied ourselves eating, he would go to his friends.

It did not take long to the finish the food. We then went into the next phase, looking out the windows and back windscreen. There would always be something happening. Drunken men and women were often comical sights to watch. These, however, turned to frightening sights when verbal abuse turned to physical brawls.

But Periappa never got into brawls. He just remained in the verbal combat stage, especially if he caught up with some of his customers who had been slow in settling their debts. But most of the time he remained light-headedly jovial.

When he finally got back to the car, he was quite a different man. His visits to the toddy shop, which could be anything between twenty minutes and an hour, usually transformed him. He would get into the car and begin his tirade against the uncaring world. But it always started with questions about my mother or Periamma. We were his audience, answering him with a word or two but only when necessary, in order to not make him angry. 'Dei, Bala, your mother told you not to go in my car, didn't she?' he would ask in Tamil.

To this I would quickly say, 'No, Periappa, Amma did not say anything like that.' This would be enough for him.

Periappa would then turn to my cousins. 'Ei, your mother, she told you not to go in Appa's car, didn't she?' he would ask accusingly. To this, my two cousins would reply in practised harmony, 'Illai, Illai, Appa. Amma did not say anything.'

What happened next depended very much on Periappa's level of intoxication and frustration (he often did not sell much cloth). As he got more engrossed in his woes, his driving would also get slightly more reckless (this was the main reason we had been instructed not to accept Periappa's invitations for rides).

Periappa would keep going onto the wrong side of the road. When he did this, too afraid to scream, we would all duck behind the front seats. Yet, he never had any accidents. He always brought us home safely, although often in a ruffled emotional state. However, we always built up enough courage for the next trip. It must have been this excitement that had drawn us to his car rides.

On our luckier days, Periappa would arrive at the Jalan San Peng toddy shop only to discover that all the drink had been sold out. He would get back into the car (we would not get any goodies) and we would be off for a long ride! We knew where he was heading. We were going to a toddy shop in Jalan Berhala. It seemed to us as that we had to drive across Kuala Lumpur to get there.

Once there, we would repeat the same routine, the only difference being that Periappa would have a little more toddy, as a reward for the extra distance he had travelled. The return journeys from this toddy shop were usually more fun as Periappa—being nearly drunk—would attempt to speak the little English he knew.

'Dei, Bala, your mother no like me,' he would start. 'I drink toddy to enjoy. Enjoy. She no like.'

Amused, embarrassed and slightly frightened, we would look out the window. But there would be no stopping him.

'Ei, bladdy fool,' he would start in English and continue his ranting in Tamil.

We were not afraid of Periappa. He would continue talking to himself, every once in a while calling out one of our names. Often it was mine. Eventually, the long, meandering car ride would come to a halt in front of Periappa's house and we would quickly run out without even a word of thanks, hoping neither my mother or Periamma spotted us.

* * *

The prayer session in the house was due to start an hour or two before the church funeral. More people came to pay their last respects. The funeral tent was almost full of men. A few of Periappa's toddy shop cronies had also turned up. Too tipsy to walk up the three flights of stairs, they remained seated in the tent. Periamma could do without their presence.

My younger brother emerged from a group of our cousins and sat next to me. He did not look very well.

'What's wrong with you?' I asked, not really wanting to know.

'Akka said we have to kiss Periappa before they close the coffin,' he said.

'What?' I almost shouted. This was our first family funeral. Kissing living members of the family would have been an ordeal enough. Kissing our dead Periappa was a definite no-no.

'I'm not kissing anybody, dead or alive,' I hissed back.

'You've no choice,' he insisted.

'I do and I won't.' I stood my ground. I imagined kissing a cold hard cheek. The knot in my stomach grew tighter and I feared I might just throw up during the very act.

My mind raced. I had to think of something to get out of this. I had given him blood. There was enough filial piety in that act for all that he had done for me. I looked out from the funeral tent unseeingly, trying to come up with an escape plan.

The old car stood where it had been parked. It could have been one of Periappa's last few acts before he died, I thought. Something about the car drew me to it. I walked casually towards it. The door to the driver's seat was not locked. Someone must have been using it. Unconsciously, I opened the door and sat at Periappa's seat. It felt strange. I had never been in the driver's seat before. I remembered ducking behind this seat when a drunk once peered at us during one of our drives with Periappa. Then I knew what I could do.

I was back in the funeral tent still feeling distracted and uncomfortable. My younger brother was nowhere in sight. That was a relief. But it was short-lived.

'Bala, Amma wants us to go upstairs. The prayer session is going to start,' my younger brother announced.

'Shit.' I muttered under my breath and followed.

The hall was in near pandemonium. Women were weeping and wailing. I did not need this. There was no way

I was going in there. I slowly made my way back to the funeral tent and moved off towards Periappa's car.

At the sound of people getting up from their chairs, I looked up through the car window, easing my crammed body from the car floor, where I had sat crouched. People were gathering around the hearse. Periappa's coffin was going to be placed in the hearse. I quickly got out of the car and moved towards the hearse. Athan spotted me and beckoned me towards him.

'Everyone was looking for you,' he started.

'I didn't want to kiss him,' I quickly added. He gave me a quizzical look but said no more.

My younger brother came and stood next to me. He did not seem to have been overly traumatized. 'Did you kiss him?' I asked.

'No, we just stood behind our cousins. They did,' he replied.

* * *

Years later, I visited Periamma to say goodbye to her. Not having seen her for many years, I was surprised by how little she seemed to have aged. She looked happier than I had ever seen her before. She told me of her many visits to my cousin's home in Australia. She had even gone to visit my sister in Canada with my mother. I was finally going to be leaving the country for the first time and she seemed to have already been everywhere!

As I got up to leave, I walked up to her and held her gently in my arms. She smiled at me, and I was her little nephew again. I kissed her.

Drowning

Lying on his hospital bed, Rama's mind wandered. He knew the dreaded time for his bath was imminent. His bath time had often moved from a feeling of drowning to that of delight. It all depended on how the water descended upon his body. Rama loved water, but only when he could control how it flowed over him. It had not always met him gently, instead, it had been thrown on him in dipper-loads.

Rama's left leg was in a cast as was his right hand. A saline drip on his left hand was hooked to a stand. He was barely able to move. Due to this, he had lost control of the privacy he had grown to treasure in his early youth and then taken for granted as he grew older. His daily hurried baths had turned to slow showers, and over the years, it had become a private ritualized daily event that he cherished. This attitude was in stark contrast to his younger self's feelings on bathing.

As a child, taking his morning bath was an unpleasant experience. Rama's family could not afford modern amenities. Water was scooped with a dipper from a concrete water-tub in a poorly lit bathroom. As a young boy during

41

his bath, his grandmother—his Paati—would scoop out cold water from the water-tub. She would hold his shoulder as she poured the water on him, and he would splutter and try to catch his breath. Without stopping, she would pour water over him, dipper-load after dipper-load. He would struggle as the water would enter his nose and mouth. Her strong hand would hold him down as he would struggle to get on his feet. His eyes would remain closed. He would move his head from side to side. He would felt the sensation of drowning and suffocation as water would enter his nose and mouth. He would struggle to breathe and gasp for air. Only when Paati would finally stop pouring the water that his panting would slowly subside. His young body would then stop shaking and she would let go of his shoulder. This sensation of feeling as though he was drowning persisted as long as someone bathed him.

Once he began primary school, his daily baths became an individual task but not a private one. Rama would quickly take off his clothes and run into the bathroom. The door would have to remain open for external supervision by Paati or Amma or any older brother who was at hand. The first few dipper-loads of cold water he would pour swiftly. His body would slowly stop shivering and he would calm down. He would then begin to soap his body. The soap bubbles that emerged on his body as he lathered himself would begin to distract him, but before it could turn to play, his name would be called, asking him to hurry. Another sibling was in the queue for his bath.

As a young boy, bathing was a hurried episode in his daily life. A twice in a day-event in the small, dark bathroom, besides the times he had to wash himself after going to the toilet. Toilet paper, he would discover in his youth. It had been drummed into him that cleanliness was a virtue, but water was to be used sparingly. Money did not grow on trees; he was constantly reminded. Piped-in water was also a new development for their family.

Thirty years later, in the privacy of his own bathroom, at the start of his morning shower, Rama would stand away from the direction of the spray of water, waiting for it to get to the temperature he desired. The running of warm water from his head, down his body, had become a sensual experience. The fear of drowning that he dreaded, as water fell upon him at the beginning of a bath, was now lost in the distant past. Now, that fear was replaced with a desire to feel the water gently run over his hair, fall on his strong shoulders, over his chest and erect nipples, still hard in the cold morning air.

Rama could hear the nurses moving outside the room he shared with three strangers. Men with broken limbs. Fortunately, none of them seemed to have incurred major injuries. They were all awake but silent. He was the one who was the least mobile. He seemed to have fared the worst among them. His helmet had protected his head, but his limbs had paid a high price.

Rama looked at the three other men in the room. One was an old Chinese man. The other two were young Malays. It was their race that he recognized at first. His fellow-sufferers shared a common predicament, broken bones. They had not spoken to each other. Rama welcomed the silence. He was not in the mood for small talk.

The scene immediately after his accident was still vivid in Rama's mind. He saw himself on his bike. It had been raining heavily and he'd ridden a little too fast. He went over running water. The next thing he knew he had hit a pot-hole and his body was being thrown off his bike, hitting the side of a lorry.

He had lain on the road in pain. The rain had continued to come down on his body. Two men were looking at him.

He heard one shout at him, '*Keling, bodoh!*'

They continued speaking in Malay, uncaring for his body lying in the middle of the road. '*Sekarang kena buat polis repot,*' he heard a voice complain.

Then he felt the once-familiar sensation of drowning slowly overwhelm him and he lost consciousness, only to wake up in the Emergency ward of a hospital.

A nurse walked into the room. Looking at Rama, he asked, 'Ready for bath?' The words took him back to his childhood and the fear of drowning returned almost instantly. No one had touched his body since his Amma or Paati last bathed him. He had no desire to have anyone help him with his bath.

'I'll bring water to get you cleaned,' the nurse said in a matter-of-fact manner.

Rama's discomfort rose. He did not want to be touched by another person, let alone by a man he did not know. His mind raced between embarrassment and anger. The motorbike accident had brought him to this state, he chided himself. His body had been covered with sweat and blood. He wanted to get rid of the clammy feeling all over his body. He consoled himself that it could have been worse, a female nurse might be attending to him.

As he lay, unready for this turn of events, the nurse brought in a low trolley with two plastic basins of water on it. He saw the liquid soap bottle, sponge and towels all neatly laid out.

The curtain was drawn around the bed and there stood the man who was going to help clean him for the first time in his adulthood. His name tag read: Malek. And below it, 'Nursing Assistant'. It did not bother Rama that Malek was a Malay.

Malek spoke when needed. He raised the top half of the bed and Rama was now in a sitting position. He informed Rama what he would do and proceeded. Soon Rama was seated naked waist upwards. Malek was all business. He started with Rama's face. The face and neck were washed with a small towel soaked with soap and water. Then rinsed with another towel. Rama felt clean. He began to relax. The drowning sensation he had anticipated had not resurfaced. Malek moved Rama's body with care and expertise, keeping Rama's discomfort to the minimum.

Rama was unsure what Malek would do next. He was despairing about how to deal with the cleaning of his private parts without feeling embarrassment and a sense of shame. The last persons who had done that for him were Paati and Amma when he was a young boy. He had never fallen ill nor needed anyone to bathe him again. His present predicament felt even worse than the drowning sensation he had once felt when Paati bathed him.

Malek moved to the other end of the bed and pushed Rama's sarong up to his groin area. He then began to sponge Rama's right leg with a small towel. Once he had completed, he asked Rama, 'You can clean yourself there?' Rama looked at both his hands. Before he could say anything, Malek said, 'I help you today'. Rama was not capable of blushing, but he certainly did feel embarrassed.

Malek loosened Rama's sarong and slowly pulled it down. Rama felt a sudden stir in his cock, exposing its head.

Malek saw it and commented, '*Tak sunat.* Dirty.' Rama could not believe what he had just heard. Malek continued with his work. He used a small damp towel to wipe Rama's private part with expert ease and dried him.

Of course, I'm not circumcised. My name is Rama. Named after Lord Rama. Which Hindu is circumcised? Dirty? Have dare you say I am unclean? '*Babi,*' he swore under his breath. He seethed with anger.

Malek was busy replacing Rama's sarong. He was completely unaware that his remark had infuriated Rama. Rama was no longer concerned with his modesty. He just wanted Malek to leave with the two basins of dirty water.

Malek's casual observation had triggered something that lay silent and deep within Rama. The constant bombardment of unwelcomed labels. He had grown weary of hearing, *tak halal, kaffir*—all these words of erasure, hurled at people like him, who were treated as outsiders despite his people having had a long history of presence in this country. Rama did not need to hear about something that was not only personal but also private.

A wave of nausea rose within him. He was unable to keep it down. His body convulsed from the pit of his stomach. He choked on his bile as it came through his nose and mouth. He felt like he was drowning all over again.

The Good Daughter

Every time I recall how my elder sister, Prema Akka, looked, my mind goes back to the last time I saw her. I must have been around eight years old. She's walking towards an aeroplane. She has hung her handbag on her shoulders, so that her hands are free, and she can wave at us. As she gets onto the first step of the stairway, she turns around and waves. She has a broad smile and her right hand is waving vigorously at us. There are no tears. I wondered then, as I do now, if she ever saw us at the terminal, waving back to her.

Prema Akka had worked very hard to leave Malaysia to further her studies. Her school certificate results had been average and she could not get into the government school Form Six classes. For two years, she worked in an office doing clerical work. She kept late hours earning good over-time wages. She saved most of the money, but she still gave a sizeable amount to my parents.

Once she had saved enough for her airfare and fees, she told my parents that she was applying for a nursing course in London. My parents did not object. They had always known of her plans and they wanted Prema to have a profession. A daughter working as a clerk would find it difficult to get a good husband. My parents loved Prema Akka and thought nursing could improve her prospects in all aspects of her life.

Prema Akka had always given them little cause for concern. She did nothing that my parents disapproved of. She went where they wanted her to and did all that they asked of her. She had even been earning a salary and was helping them financially. And above all this, she did most of the household chores. Her obedience did not go unobserved. Our neighbours complimented my mother on her excellent upbringing of her daughter. They often praised Prema Akka and gave her what they considered the ultimate compliment—one day she will make an excellent wife to some lucky young man.

* * *

Twelve years is a long time and a younger brother does forget how his sister actually looks. Although I still see that image of Prema Akka at the airport, the picture is rather blurred and I am no longer sure what she looks like. All the photos we have of her in the house were taken before she left for England, with a few shots of her first few years there.

Prema Akka kept in touch with us regularly. We received a brief letter from her every fortnight, informing us that she was well. The only time she telephoned was on Deepavali. She would talk to my father, then my mother, and finally me. We said little to each other. It was often a greeting, how are you, and please ask Amma to give you ten Ringgit for your Deepavali present from me.

While she was still a student nurse, Prema Akka would send some money whenever she could. Once she was a qualified staff nurse, she reverted to her old wage-earning self and sent my parents money every month. My parents proudly took their monthly bank draft to the nearby bank and deposited it. This piece of news soon spread in the neighbourhood. Within a few months, our neighbours were saying what a good daughter Prema Akka was. My parents beamed from ear to ear.

Soon proposals of marriage for Prema Akka arrived at our doorstep. My parents informed the families that Prema Akka would be back soon and once she gets a job at a local hospital, they would talk to her about marriage. Just about the same time, Prema Akka informed my parents she was staying on for another year to do specialist training. Then each following year, she would give yet another reason for her postponed return to Malaysia.

My parents were disappointed but never got angry. They then took another approach with Prema Akka. They asked her to come back for a holiday. Prema Akka never said 'no'. She would always reply saying she will try. Then, she would write and say that work was hectic and it was difficult to take leave for more than a few days at a stretch. The bank drafts only got bigger and my parents found it difficult to complain. Now, fewer people asked my parents about Prema Akka's return to Malaysia. Her monthly bank drafts kept tongues from wagging. It was still a symbol of Prema Akka being filial.

* * *

Amidst all this, I had written to Prema Akka asking for her help to further my studies in England. My parents had agreed to pay my airfare and some of the fees. I asked Prema Akka if she could help pay the rest of the tuition. I promised to do some part-time work to help meet my living expenses. True to everyone's expectations, she agreed. I got a place at Sheffield University and I accepted the offer.

As the days grew closer for my flight to London, my parents constantly bombarded me with advice. I was to keep away from people who smoked cigarettes and went to parties. I must remember not to eat beef. And most of all, I should not fall in love with a white girl. My father, repeatedly said, 'You must come back and marry a Tamil girl. Do not fall in love with a white girl. When she is angry, she will call you a bastard'. I was never sure how all these connected, but I dutifully listened to what my father had to say.

Then for the first time, I heard my father say something which came closest to a reprimand of Prema Akka's behaviour. 'Don't be like your Prema Akka and stay back in England after your studies. You're our *only* son. Come back and look after us in our old age,' my father said. There was hurt in my father's voice that I had not heard before.

'I'm sure Akka will come back soon. Maybe, she'll wait till I finish my studies and we will both come back to Malaysia together,' I replied.

'You talk to her when you see her,' my father said and then got up and left the room.

Clearly my father had no more to say on the matter. I began to wonder about my sister's long absence. I had assumed that Prema Akka would eventually return when she had made enough money, or had gotten enough work experience. Now, she was going to support me financially. There was little chance that she would return before I finished my studies.

My last few days in Malaysia before my flight were full of farewell dinners at our neighbours' homes. My parents and

I were invited to homes of friends who had known me from the time of my birth. I was subjected to stories of my childhood antics and misadventures. And in all these homes, there was frequent reference to Prema Akka. They all started by saying what a good daughter she has been, helping my parents by sending home money every month. Then, unfailingly, they would all ask me to tell her to come back to Malaysia soon. Their lines were almost identical: your parents are old, Prema Akka is no longer young, she needs to get married and finally, my parents must see some grandchildren soon.

* * *

'Ravi!' I heard someone call my name. I turned around, expecting to see my sister with long, plaited hair. It was quite a different person who had called my name. She looked lovely in shoulder length hair. I could tell that she was my sister. The eyes and smile were still familiar. But nothing else resembled the sister I had seen more than ten years ago.

'Prema Akka?' I still asked.

'Yes, you silly goose,' she replied and hugged me.

She was my sister all right! Her favourite expression had been 'silly goose' and apparently still was. I was not used to this hugging. We shook hands when we said goodbye years ago at the airport. I felt awkward being hugged. But it was a pleasant awkwardness, after the thirteen-hour long flight that hadn't been unpleasant but neither was it comfortable. I wanted to go to the toilet to pee about halfway through the flight but was just too afraid to do so. I had seen people queuing and was afraid to embarrass myself, fearing someone might open the door while I was still at it.

We made our way towards a train station and then to her house. Heathrow Airport was huge and I allowed her to take charge. We changed trains and I found myself in her two-bedroom house. It was good to be in a warm room again. It was late September and cold for me. It was not quite evening but it was already getting dark.

Prema Akka made me a warm mug of Milo. I was glad to be with my sister. She was being good to me. I told her about our parents and all the people who had asked after her. Some names made an impression on her but the others did not. However, I didn't quite relate their actual messages. I didn't think it was the appropriate time or even my place to do so. But I did tell her that Amma and Appa missed her very much and hoped that she would at least visit them.

'Ravi, we'll talk about all that later. You silly goose, you just got here and you want me to go back to Malaysia!' she laughed away the matter.

I gave her my parents' gifts. She broke into a wide smile. I was happy to see her genuinely happy. It was different from her earlier laughter.

'Akka, why did you never come back to visit us?' I asked earnestly.

She sighed. There was a long silence. Then she replied, 'Ravi, it is a long story. I have to work in a couple of hours. Let's talk about this later.'

'I have to leave for Sheffield in a few days,' I told her. I did not mean that we should continue on the topic of her staying so long in England.

'Anyway, you're here for another three years. Lots of time to talk,' she added.

'No, not that, I just wanted to know how to get myself organized to go to the university,' I replied.

This time she laughed at herself. 'No, problem, David and I can drive you there,' she explained.

'Who's David?' I asked in sheer reflex.

She sighed again. 'Ravi, David's my partner. He's something like a boyfriend . . . just that it is on a more permanent basis. We're not married. We've been living together for the last three years.'

'He won't let you go back to Malaysia?' I asked as anger at this man rose within me.

'No, David is not the reason. I chose to stay back. He's a good man.' Prema Akka was quick to reply. I wanted to know more on what was keeping her from going back home to Malaysia.

'So why don't you both go back home? Some of our parent's friends' children have married outside our race and they have returned home.'

'Well, that's where the problem lies. I'm not married and we're not going to get married, either.'

'Just tell Amma and Appa you're married. They're not going to ask for the marriage certificate!'

'Ravi, stop. You just got here. You just have to accept for now that I can't go back. I cannot lie to them. They have expectations of me. I don't want to break their hearts.'

* * *

I was lying on my bed, trying to sleep when I heard someone walk into the house. I knew it must be David. I wasn't sure

what I should do. Did he expect me to come out and greet
him? He wasn't exactly my brother-in-law. I didn't even know
if I was staying in *his* house. While I was lost in my thoughts,
I heard him open and shut another door. I assumed he had
gone into the other bedroom.

A little later, I heard him again. He had gone downstairs.
I felt uneasy lying on the bed listening to the sounds he was
making. I got out of bed and went downstairs. I found him in
the kitchen. He was not the middle-aged man I had expected
to meet. He looked well past his fifties. I decided to play it
safe and just introduce myself.

'Hi! I'm David,' he replied.

My heart sank. My sister was living with this old man.
Whatever made her choose him? I wondered.

David was very pleasant. He invited me to have dinner
with him, which I declined. I told him I'd wait for my sister.
He asked me about my flight and went on to ask my plans for
Sheffield. He offered me a can of beer which I was tempted
to accept, but ultimately declined. I agreed to a cup of tea.

David joked about Prema Akka buying a can of Milo just
in case I did not drink coffee or tea. She had remembered
that I loved drinking Milo as a child. Suddenly, I felt tired. I
decided to catch with my sleep. I asked David to let Prema
Akka know that I would have to skip dinner. We bid each
other good night and I went back to my bedroom.

The barking of dogs awoke me. I looked out the window.
It was already morning. I felt rested. I remembered talking to
David. He did seem like a good guy. I went downstairs and
found no one. I went up to my sister's bedroom and knocked.
There was no reply. The door actually opened. I walked
into the room. I didn't think I was intruding. The door was

not locked. It was a lovely room. Everything seemed to be in its place. The dressing table was immaculately arranged. There were two photographs on it. There was one of Prema Akka and David. The other was that of a very young child. I could not make out whether it was a boy or a girl.

* * *

'Ravi, you should not just go into other people's rooms,' Prema Akka told me with some irritation.

'I knocked and the door opened. I really did not think I was intruding. I was out of there in a minute. I'm not sure why you're getting so upset. At home, we went into everyone's room. Amma comes into my room even when I'm in it. I'm not even allowed to lock the door. Anyway, all I asked was who is that child in the photograph?'

Prema Akka let out a long sigh this time. Then she said what I was not quite ready for.

'Well, Ravi, that's the photograph of your nephew, James Kumar,' my sister replied.

Before I could say anything, she continued, 'Kumar is four years old. He's not here in his home because he's not well. He is a lovely child. He's just not well.' Her voice grew sad and I felt sorry and puzzled at the same time.

'Akka, you have a son and you never told us. Why did you ask me to come here when there were so many things you were keeping from us?'

'Ravi, I did not mean to keep anything from anyone. I met David at a time when I needed an anchor in my life. He gave me that strength. I fell in love. I did not think it wrong. I just did not know how to tell Amma and Appa. David does not want to get married and I can't force him. Then Kumar arrived. He was such a lively child. But three months ago he suddenly developed brain fever. He almost died. Just when the doctors had given up all hope, he came back to us. But his little brain had been badly damaged. His heart continues to beat but his other organs are also beginning to fail. He looks at me but does not see me. Sometimes he seems to respond to some sounds, at other times, he lies there just staring blankly.'

I was lost for words. My sister has a family back home in Malaysia but could not draw their support. I knew my family would not be accepting of Prema Akka's relationship, and a child born out of wedlock would further complicate her situation. I stared blankly at Prema Akka, feeling rather helpless.

'I have him in a private nursing home. There is trained staff to attend to him. He will not see this year through. His death will be the price I will pay for my sins. I wish there was some other way. When I was pregnant, I thought it fate that I conceived. A blessing. I was *not* wrong. I had four wonderful years with him. I'm losing him now. It is fate, too. David is the father and he's been here for both of us.'

I was lost for words. I got up from my chair and walked towards my sister. This time I held her in my arms.

* * *

I had settled into my room in Sheffield. There were eight of us in this two-bedroom house. We joked about how our body heat kept this cold house warm. I decided I would not write to Appa and Amma to tell them about Prema Akka. Kumar had died three weeks after I left London. I'm not sure how Prema Akka felt about his death. She rang to let me know that my nephew had died. She told me I need not come to the crematorium. She said it will be just David and her. I thought it was appropriate. It had always been the three of them.

My first semester in Sheffield was going alright. I had spoken to Prema Akka a few days ago and agreed to spend my Christmas holidays with her. I cannot claim to understand my sister. In agreeing to pay for my fees, she had invited me into her life again. She had finally shared her joy and her sorrow with me. Yet they were hers alone. I had remained largely in the periphery for most of her life. I hope I will not remain there long. I want to be her brother again.

Brother Felix's Ward

Johan sat very still. His head was bowed low. His fingers were clasped together tightly. As he heard Brother Felix say 'Amen', his fingers relaxed and slowly disengaged. He slowly raised his head. He saw Brother Felix's radiant, happy, glowing face. Brother Felix's gaze fell on him and he seemed to smile a little wider. The other boys were already leaving their seats. Johan wanted to linger for a little while longer. He felt a calmness within him. Johan knew where he ought to be. He slowly made his way out of the chapel and headed to the mosque. Today, he had lingered a little longer than he should have.

Johan knew he was not supposed to attend Chapel. At the sound of the last bell on Fridays, his Muslim classmates would leave school and head for lunch or sometimes go directly to the mosque for Friday prayers. Johan was a loner and did not go with his classmates. They found him aloof and different. Soon, they found out that he went to the chapel in school before going to the mosque for Friday prayers.

They were amused and did not care what Johan did. They did not even say anything to the adults.

When his first year at his new school ended, Johan longed to attend Friday Chapel. Johan yearned for the music, the songs and the stories he heard each week. When Brother Felix mentioned certain prophets, he would recognize them as Adam, Ibrahim, Musa and most of all, Nabi Isa. He had been taught about all of them by his *Al-Quran* and *Fardu Ain* teachers.

Brother Felix had often talked about Jesus or Nabi Isa, as Johan had first known of him. Johan did not tire hearing stories of Jesus' miracles or of the parables with their teachings. Soon Jesus was rarely Isa to Johan. He did not go beyond these stories. Johan did not want to hear about the Jesus who was crucified and was said to have risen. He did not want to hear about the Jesus who was resurrected from the dead and whom the Christians called God. The Jesus that was alive and preaching love was enough for him.

Johan was drawn to Jesus, the man. He was drawn to Brother Felix. Brother Felix told the stories that Jesus had. Stories about love, kindness and forgiveness. Soon, Johan wanted to be like Brother Felix. His young mind could not have comprehended the ramifications of his desire. Johan did not see in his young, innocent mind the transgressions he would be making by merely desiring to be like Brother Felix.

* * *

Brother Felix treated Johan as he did all the young boys under his care. He was aware of the complex and complicated racial and religious situation in the newly formed Malaysia.

He was glad that a missionary school like his could continue to operate in a Muslim country.

Brother Felix had enjoyed playing football as a young man and continued to play when he found the time. He had broad shoulders and a well-built body, akin to what one would see on soldiers. He was strong and felt ready to go to a distant country in Asia. Brother Felix had heard his calling to come to Malaysia in his thirties. He did not have to wait long. One of the other Brothers who had just returned from a short stint in Malaysia had informed him of a teaching position in a secondary school in Malacca and he had immediately applied for it.

He arrived in Singapore and made his way to Malacca. He was welcomed by the other Brothers and Sisters who were already there in this small town. He was to teach English in the only school set up for boys by the Catholic church. His first day of teaching went by quite uneventfully. What struck him were the different colours of his students. They were certainly quite different from those in Dublin. However, the colours meant little to Brother Felix. They were all the same in his flock.

It did not take long for Brother Felix to discover that they were certainly not the same and a few had to be treated slightly differently. In his induction to Malaysian life, Brother Felix discovered the religious mosaic of the country. The main concerns were to be with the Muslim students. They were to be set apart and given different religious instruction in the Catholic School. Brother Paul, the Headmaster, had been very clear about it when he had met Brother Felix for the first time. Brother Paul, now in his late fifties, had arrived on Malayan shores just like Brother Felix. Over the two decades that he'd been here, he had learned the ways of the local authorities and adapted accordingly. 'There will be no preaching or conversion of Muslim students to Christianity,' Brother Paul had instructed Brother Felix. That would be at the peril of closing down this school and the Brothers' Provincialate. The La Sallian Brothers certainly did not want that to befall them, he was explicitly cautioned.

Brother Felix, however, wondered why Muslim parents would want their children to attend a missionary school. A local teacher gave him the answer. One day, a young twenty-something Chinese English language teacher, Miss Esther Lim, informed him, 'They want their children to learn English well and be able to go overseas for further studies.' With that Brother Felix's lessons on Malaysia and Malaysians, especially Muslim Malaysians, had slowly begun. It was made clear to him that Christianity was out of bounds for Malay boys in missionary schools. There was no compromise on this matter, none whatsoever.

Brother Felix was in his eighth year of teaching when Johan joined the school in a Form Two class. He was a precocious young boy. Johan was in Brother Felix's English language class. Johan was a keen reader, and his language proficiency was the highest among his peers. Johan had breezed through Enid Blyton stories and gone on to the more modern Hardy Boys mysteries. Brother Felix could not help but take notice of this young boy. He wrote excellent compositions but spoke only when called to answer a question. Johan did not enjoy sports, and this kept him very much on his own. He chose to sit in the last row in the class and was often by himself.

Johan was a fair-skinned lad. His facial features were not typically Malay. When he spoke, it was always in English. He looked like some of the Eurasian boys in the school. Johan did not join the Malay boys in his class, either. They spoke both English and Malay but seemed unwelcoming towards this new kid who spoke only in English. Most people did not think him to be Malay. Brother Felix was one of those who did not think of Johan to be Malay either, until he saw the young man's full name in the class register.

Brother Felix was given the task of conducting the weekly lessons from the Bible during Chapel in the chapel. The students arrived for the sessions with mixed feelings. Most did not seem to want be there. It took a while for them to settle down. The other Brothers were present to help the boys settle down. Soon the chapel was almost full. Johan was among the last to enter the chapel and as usual, he sat alone and in the last pew. Brother Felix only noticed Johan after a few Fridays. Just as in the English Language class, Johan sat there quietly, listening with a faraway look. Lost in his own world. Brother Felix chose not to say anything.

Johan listened to Brother Felix's Bible stories but rarely waited for the moral lessons that followed. His attention would wane as the stories drew to a close and as soon as the pedantic part began, his mind would switch off and he would quietly slip away before the others could notice him.

Johan's thoughts often lingered on the stories he had heard during Chapel. Many of these stories he had heard before about prophet Ibrahim and Ishak, Musa and Adam. Just the names had been changed here. He was fascinated when he heard the stories that Jesus had told. Johan understood sibling rivalry and envy in the tale about the prodigal son. In his gentle heart, he sought to emulate the kindness of the good Samaritan. These were new stories to him.

A desire slowly began to grow in Johan. He wanted to read and hear more about this gentle prophet who preached love and was later scorned by some of his own people and the Romans. Johan scoured a few history books in the school library and found the historical Jesus mentioned in passing. Then one day, by sheer chance he found a Bible stories series in the fiction section. And over the next few weeks, he managed to read the twenty-five titles in the whole series.

* * *

Brother Felix prepared for his English language classes with the same enthusiasm he prepared for Chapel. In both, Johan remained seated at the back and Brother Felix thought it best to leave the boy alone. He sensed Johan was different and he was not sure if there was something that was troubling the lad.

During the double-period English language classes, which were towards the end of a long school day, Brother Felix would play a game with the students. He would tell them a story and ask them to give an ending or ask the students to give a lesson they could learn from the story. These stories were short enough to hold their attention and the class would listen intently. The students would respond rather enthusiastically, especially once they knew that someone would get a small prize from Brother Felix. Johan listened intently like the others. He enjoyed the stories and knew the lessons they taught. He had read many of them in the books on the library shelves. His heart warmed when he heard Brother Felix now re-tell these stories. Yet, Johan felt no desire to raise his hand in class to answer Brother Felix's questions. Hearing the stories from Brother Felix were gifts enough. He also did not want to draw any attention to himself.

Soon there were only a few more weeks before public examinations. Johan and his classmates were busy with their preparations for the examinations. The school Chapel sessions continued as usual. One Friday, just as Johan was slipping away from the chapel and rushing off to the mosque for the prayers, his Bahasa Malaysia teacher saw him. The teacher called him aside and asked Johan what he was doing coming out from the chapel.

'Listening to the Bible stories, sir,' he replied in Malay.

The teacher gave him a stern warning, 'Stop going to the chapel. It is not for you. If you go again, your parents will be informed.'

Johan nodded, thanked his teacher, and fled. He knew why the teacher forbade him to go to the chapel. It broke his heart that he had been caught. He sobbed all the way to the mosque, knowing he could not return to the chapel anymore. His mind was troubled throughout the Friday prayers. He found it hard to pay attention to the sermon that was being preached. As the prayers drew to a close and the worshippers began to leave, Johan remained seated in his place. His eyes were closed, and he tried to clear his mind. But the troubling words from his Bahasa Malaysia teacher continued to ring loudly in his head. After a few minutes, finding no solace, he got up and left for home.

* * *

Johan was back at his seat in his classroom on Monday. Classes went on as usual. Brother Felix was his usual self, completely unaware of what had transpired on Friday. The Bahasa Malaysia teacher came to class and taught his lesson. Just as the bell rang, and Johan was about to sigh with relief, the teacher called out Johan's name and said, '*Johan, jangan lupa apa yang saya kata pada kamu,*' reminding Johan of his warning. His classmates, however, paid no heed to what the teacher had told Johan.

As Friday drew close, Johan longed to go to Chapel. He had grown accustomed to it. The whole of that Friday morning, a struggle raged within him. He could not see the problem in attending Friday Chapel, then rushing off for Friday prayers. Attending Chapel had not turned him away from his religion. After the final class on Friday, Johan walked slowly to the mosque. He knew the chapel routine well and that by the time he reached the mosque, Brother Felix would be giving his weekly lesson to his schoolmates. Johan did his ablutions and joined the men in the mosque.

The last week of class finally arrived. There were a few revision lessons and 'spotting' of exam questions for the examination. Brother Felix walked into the classroom with his usual bright smile. Johan knew that this would be the final class with Brother Felix. They were going to have a few days of study leave before the examination began the following week. Like the other teachers, Brother Felix also gave tips for the examinations. Unlike his regular way of ending lessons, today, Brother Felix had no time for a story for his students. He ended his class in an unusual manner. He looked at all his students and bid them farewell, 'You have my best wishes and God bless each one of you.' He beamed at the students, picked up his books, and waited for their practised reply. The students shouted out, 'Thank you, Brother Felix.'

Johan felt a sadness descend upon him. He saw the end of something he had treasured. This second year in the new school had been trying. His parents had demanded excellent grades from him so that he could enter the Science stream the next year, in a new school overseas. Brother Felix had been a beacon in his lonely life. English language classes had not just been about learning the English language but also about listening to Brother Felix's Bible stories, narrated in his calming voice.

He remembered his English language teacher from the previous school. Puan Halimah taught English using so many Malay words that it frustrated Johan. He felt his Bahasa Malaysia improving, but not his English. His classmates were generally weak in English and were quite happy with Puan Halimah's style of teaching. Johan's parents wanted more for him and got him transferred out of the school.

Johan knew this day would come. It had been scheduled and was expected. Not the way his attending Chapel had suddenly been terminated. That had been unexpected and painful. He thought it cruel, even. He felt as though something he enjoyed and loved had been snatched away from him. His young mind was completely oblivious to what could have happened if his Bahasa Malaysia teacher had made a complaint to the religious authorities.

Johan wanted to see Brother Felix. He wanted to say thank you for all that Brother Felix had done for him. Johan feared he may not see Brother Felix again, unsure as he was about when he would be leaving for England.

* * *

Johan knocked on Brother Felix's office door. On the door, he saw Brother Felix's name and job designation. It read, 'Brother Felix' and beneath it, 'Senior Assistant'. A familiar voice answered, 'Come in.' Brother Felix was seated at his table. Johan had never been into this office. Brother Felix gave him his familiar warm smile.

'Ah, Johan! Wasn't expecting you to come see me. Sit down.'

'Good afternoon, Brother Felix,' Johan replied.

Johan sat on the chair in front of Brother Felix.

'Sir, I wanted to come and thank you,' he said.

Brother Felix was not accustomed to having students drop by his office to thank him. Most shied away from his office and some dreaded being called to see him as it often meant that some disciplinary issue needed to be addressed.

'Johan, it's been a pleasure teaching you. You should speak up more in class,' Brother Felix said.

'Brother Felix, I really liked your stories, too.'

'They are not my stories, they are stories from the Bible, Johan.'

'Sir, I know. I read a few in the library . . . Brother Felix, could you give me a copy of the Bible?' Johan asked. Johan could not believe what he had just said. He had merely come to thank his English language teacher. And now, he had blurted out a request for a copy of the Bible.

Brother Felix sat in front of Johan with the most perplexed look. No student had ever asked him for a Bible. And there sat in front of him a Muslim boy asking for a Bible. Brother Felix remembered Brother Paul's words, 'There will be no preaching or conversion of Muslim students to Christianity.'

Johan sensed a change come upon his favourite teacher's face. There was no anger there. Just some confusion and a sense of sadness.

'Brother Felix, I'm not sure why I suddenly asked you for a Bible. I just came to say thank you for the English classes and for the stories during Chapel on Fridays. I will miss both.'

Johan quickly got up, gave Brother Felix a bow and fled from his office. Anyone seeing Johan leave Brother Felix's office would have thought that he had just received a punishment from the school's Senior Assistant.

Brother Felix sat at his table for a long time thinking of Johan and all his wards. He began to weep silently.

Coitus Interruptus

Kumar led Sunitha through the bedroom doors. Before she knew what was happening, he had already unzipped her dress. She felt it slip over her shoulders and fall on the floor. She stood unmoving while he unbuckled her bra and soon she stood completely naked. She turned around and looked at him. He had also begun undressing and she could clearly sense his excitement. He led her to the bed and almost immediately, he was pressing his body over hers.

He kissed her fervently on her lips and breasts. She responded gently. She felt his hands part her legs. He began to move his body against hers. She was not ready for him but he was insistent. She tried to push his hands aside. She wanted him to slow down. He was unwavering. He parted her legs again and placed himself upon her. She began to struggle.

She felt him trying to force himself into her. She tried to push him away. His lips were hard upon her mouth and she could not speak. He pushed against her, and she felt him enter her. She tried to scream as pain ripped through her body. He was now completely inside her. He suddenly stopped. Her body relaxed. She felt the tears on her cheeks.

Kumar took her body relaxing as consent. He continued his thrusting. Sunitha felt her pain slowly disappear and a sensation of pleasure she had not felt before began to rise within her. Her body began to respond to his body. She held him tightly. She began to enjoy Kumar inside her. Kumar continued his urgent strokes and then, all of a sudden, he pulled out of her. As he lay next to her, she saw his wetness on his thighs. He moved closer to her and held her gently. '*Coitus interruptus*,' he sheepishly said to her.

Sunitha was not sure what to make of the sex. She had first felt as if it was rape, but now she was not sure. She had enjoyed it and wanted to feel him inside her again.

She did. He had Sunitha in the same way the following week, and many more weeks to come.

* * *

Here I go again, Sunitha thought to herself. She generally enjoyed her Saturday afternoon tea with her three friends. The traffic was bearable. As she took the exit into Subang Jaya, she remembered that she had to buy some *kueh*.

Sunitha checked the time. She was not late. The others would have arrived by now. They all lived in Subang Jaya. Zaitun would have driven to Vas's house. Malar's husband would have dropped her off on his way to take their son for his taekwondo class. Vasantha's daughter would have gone with them. It was a convenient arrangement for all. Vasantha's house had been the obvious choice for their Saturday tea sessions. Her husband worked late even on Saturdays and the four women had the whole house to themselves.

As Sunitha drew up to a road-side stall, she realized that she would have to wait before she got her order. This makcik's *goreng pisang* was excellent, she reminded herself. She had once stopped to buy some a few months back and now she returned at least once a fortnight. The old Malay woman recognized her. She was pleased.

Vasantha's Sri Lankan maid was already walking towards the gate as Sunitha got out of her car. Sunitha was greeted with a shy smile. As Sunitha walked towards the house, the maid locked the gate. *Looks like we're all here*, she thought to herself.

* * *

'Here's Sunitha and her goreng pisang,' Vasantha informed the others.

'*Yepperdi savvekiiam mah?*' Sunitha greeted the three women in Vasantha's dining room in her regular fashion. There were smiles and nods all round.

'Hei, Sunitha, why you like bananas so much?' Malar teased.

Before she could reply, Vasantha cut in, 'She doesn't get it lah! That's why.' The two women laughed at her. Sunitha wasn't very amused.

'Thanks, Vas.'

'You're welcome. Just my way of reminding you that you should say yes to Dr Kumar,' Vasantha added.

'Hei, don't start, okay? I just got here. Let's have some tea and talk about life. Death can come later.'

'Mustn't say like that,' Zaitun added rather solemnly, finally joining in the conversation.

'Just kidding, Zaitun,' Sunitha half-apologized.

The women sat in their usual places at the dining table. They were soon busy serving each other the goodies they had brought. 'Better eat the goreng pisang first. When it gets cold, it goes all soft and oily,' Sunitha joked, but regretted it the second she finished her sentence. Malar and Vasantha made funny noises. Sunitha sensed that they were bent on teasing her. Zaitun sipped her tea quietly. *Everyone is in their element*, Sunitha thought. Then quickly added, 'Will you two stop it? I know it's difficult, but surely there is more to life than talking about men and sex.'

'Who said anything about sex?' Vasantha asked accusingly. 'We get enough and we don't need to talk about it.'

'And what makes you think I don't get any?' Sunitha asked, deciding she would shock her smug friends.

'Oohh!' Vasantha and Malar cooed together.

'Our modern girl does not believe that sex should be saved up for our *Athans*.'

'Vas, you believe her, ah? She's just trying show off. Pretending to be so liberal.' Malar turned to Zaitun to say something and noticed what had happened. 'Now look what you've done to poor Zaitun,' Malar said and went into fits of laughter. Zaitun sat quietly wiping the tea she had on her cheeks.

Sunitha, deciding to take advantage of the shift in attention, asked Zaitun if everything was all right. To everyone's surprise, Zaitun burst into tears. The women gathered around her, each saying something to soothe their friend. They were accustomed to Zaitun's presence, always quiet. That was her way. The emotional outburst was right out of character.

'Mazlan wants to divor—' Zaitun could not continue. She was now weeping. Sunitha held Zaitun tight and, as she thought of Mazlan, anger welled up within her and her hold on Zaitun's arms became even stronger. *Bloody bastard*, she thought to herself.

* * *

What a disastrous Saturday, Sunitha thought. It was supposed to have been a pleasant afternoon. *We were supposed to sit around and have some silly girl talk.* Then the bombshell from Zaitun. *Poor, poor Zaitun.* It had to happen to her of course. It happens so often to the defenceless women. *Do they sit out there and send out signals, we're easy targets, hurt us, walk all over us,* Sunitha wondered. And my dear friends want me to get married. Join their league of married women. Not a good idea. *Thanks, girls, but I'll pass for now.*

Vas's husband was never around. She was the second wife, his work was clearly the first. Vas spent much of her life waiting for him. Malar's seemed a happy marriage. They seemed to be doing all right. *Hope there aren't any skeletons like Zaitun's in their closets!* Malar and Pandian had three children, their own house, and even two cars. They had money. All of Malar's energies were spent on her house, children, husband and family. She never complained and it seemed to work for her.

Would I want a marriage like Malar's?

Actually, no.

Where did Malar fit into her marriage and family?

Sunitha could have settled for what Malar had, she knew. She'd had such an offer a few years ago, but she had turned down the marriage proposal.

Who would have guessed Zaitun's marriage was on the rocks? Zaitun and Mazlan's marriage seemed as if it was working all right. Mazlan and Zaitun did things together and seemed to have a good time. Seven years of marriage had brought them no children. Here lay their problem. *Surely not cause enough for divorce.* They had vowed to love each other *not* to create little Mazlans or Zaituns. So, if they do have a problem . . . so do millions of others. Mazlan had decided it was Zaitun's fault. *How convenient.*

Sunitha wondered if any woman had divorced her husband on account of his infertility. *That would make such a change*, she smiled at her thought.

Zaitun had never coaxed or cajoled Sunitha to get married. She had been quiet on that subject too. She had never pretended her marriage was bliss and advised Sunitha that she, too, should seek a similar fate. Zaitun was a true friend. She had never attempted to impose her view on Sunitha. Sunitha believed that one has no rights with friends, only privileges that were earned. Sunitha felt she had no right to tell Zaitun what to do. But if Zaitun chose her to bare her heart to, she would listen and suggest any action when asked. That too with caution. She had long decided honesty was overrated.

Sunitha drove into the parking lot in Kumar's apartment block. She knew exactly what would happen once she got there.

* * *

Sunitha was not unfamiliar with men. Over the years, she had learned to love a few. Sunitha liked men. She thought of them as fun to have around. Yet she would not want to latch onto one for a whole day or allow a man to hang around her twenty-four hours a day, three hundred and sixty-five days a year. She needed space and she wanted a man who would give her that space.

The last time Sunitha had fallen in love, it was with David Wong. He was good fun. He rarely spoke of marriage but often spoke of love. They saw each other two to three times a week. She had happily gone to bed with him. She thought she had found in David a man who would accept her for what she was. All was well till he proposed and laid out his plans for her life. That was when it all began to go wrong. She felt she was being fitted into another person's life. Having to lose herself completely to exist in a space allocated for her. She declined his proposal and beautiful diamond ring. This clearly surprised him. He thought he was taking her away from the drudgery of teaching, not offering another prison.

'Everything will be provided for,' David declared. 'You won't have to work. You'll be a woman of leisure. You can re-decorate my bungalow. No report books to write. No more headmasters' asses to kiss.' He told her of the things she could do. All of which she would have to do alone. None of which she wanted to do with him.

Sunitha said 'no' with a heavy heart. She had liked David. No, that was not quite true. She had loved him. She still did. But she had discovered that she could not give up herself to become his wife. He could have been an interesting husband, if he wasn't so rich and peculiarly conservative. She could not subject herself to day after day of the same routine. *I'll end up just like Vas, Malar, and Zaitun. The Saturday evening tea will be the highlight of week and my life too!*

I would despair.

Sunitha was glad she had said 'no' to David and the life he had offered her. She was happy. She knew what she wanted. She was working to get it. She knew she would succeed. Sunitha had set her sights on getting out of her present world. She was going to do it on her own terms. Her plans lay close to her heart. She was not going to tell anyone. Not yet, anyway.

* * *

Driving home from Kumar's Sunitha felt happy. The sex had been good, as it often was. She had quickly learned some tricks that turned him on and capitalized on them. She realized that she enjoyed the rough play as much as he did. Despite what seemed like a lack of foreplay, Sunitha devised ways to extend their sexual activity (she never saw it as love-making). She teased him and made sure she got her pleasure too.

However, Sunitha was not sure how long their relationship would continue. She had declined Kumar's proposal of marriage the previous week. She was not completely surprised when Kumar popped the marriage question. She had not said 'yes' to a man who had loved her. She was not going to say 'yes' to another who had just indicated *interest* in her. Love had not even been mentioned. She was glad for it. It made it easier for her to say 'no'. Kumar was great company. Going out with him was fun. But marriage now seemed like a trap. Sex with him was great but she was not interested in setting up house with anyone, no matter how good a prospect he might present.

Vasantha had advised her to act fast. He would only wait so long, she had warned. Women have to choose quickly, or men slip away. *Ah well*, she thought. *There'll be others. Didn't someone say that men were like buses? Miss one and another comes along five minutes later. Anyway, I'm neither unattractive nor old*, she told herself.

Malar had been more persistent. 'Make up your mind, girl. People will talk.' Those were often her opening lines. 'He's a doctor. What's more, he's not that young, either. Get engaged at least,' she had suggested. 'Say yes. Then he'll be off the marriage circuit. People will see you as a couple. He's yours for sure. Once you're engaged, love will follow. All this *khathal* business is just the icing on the cake. Take the cake before someone else decides to taste it.' Whenever Malar felt she was losing Sunitha's attention, she would resort to fear-mongering, 'You'll short change yourself, Sunitha. No man will want to marry you if you go out so much with one man and then change your mind.'

* * *

Another Saturday arrived and Sunitha found herself early at Vasantha's front gate. She had broken all tradition and bought a few slices of pineapple instead of her usual *kueh* for their tea.

'Hei, Sunitha, what's this, ah? Just because we teased you about goreng pisang you decided to bring pineapple instead, ah?' Vasantha started on her.

'Having problems, ah?' Malar hinted knowingly.

'You two have nothing else to talk about, yah? Let's change the subject before Zaitun arrives. She is coming, isn't she?'

'Yeah. She should be here soon.'

'How is she? Heard anything more?'

'Hei, Sunitha, we have quite a lot of things to do, you know. Just because we're housewives doesn't mean we sit in the house, shake legs, and talk on the phone all day,' Malar chipped in.

'I never implied that,' Sunitha said.

'Let's start,' Vasantha suggested.

'I'll just have the pineapple, if you don't mind.'

'Not even tea?'

'Of course, I'll have a cup,' Sunitha responded, with false exasperation at Vasantha.

'Sunitha, you went out with Dr Kumar last night, ah?' Malar began.

'Must not be so nosey, Malar, you know Sunitha doesn't like us to talk about her and Dr Kumar.'

'Why? I just want know what. Maybe something happened. Sunitha, you said yes or not?'

'Malar, you won't quit, will you? If you get an invitation card, then you'll know there's an engagement!'

By five o'clock the three women had decided that Zaitun was not going to show up. Malar's husband was soon at the gate. Sunitha took her leave with Malar too.

* * *

Driving to the Royal Selangor Club, Sunitha hoped the evening with Kumar was going to be more fun than the tea had been with her girlfriends. Zaitun's absence had cast a pall over the women's meeting. She rarely stayed away. Clearly things were not going well for her. Sunitha made a mental note to call her.

Just as she was getting out of her car, she saw Kumar coming from his. They caught up with each other and walked into the club, hand in hand.

'I need a *teh-tarik*,' he said.

'Great, I feel like one, too.'

They walked towards the hawkers' stalls set up in the club. *How terribly posh*, she thought. *We come to Selangor Club for teh-tarik. The mamak-stall further down the road would probably be better and definitely cheaper. But we never go there; Kumar just didn't do that sort of thing.* Being with Kumar was always going to be like this, she decided.

After their tea, they decided they would do a slow drive along Taman Perdana and go to his apartment in Damansara. Sunitha wanted the evening to end on a high note.

Now as she lay with her head on Kumar's chest, as she had done so many times before, Sunitha wondered how many more times she would be invited to his bed before their relationship ended. She knew he would want to get married. Indian mothers wanted that, and good Indian sons usually obliged their mummies. In her mind, Sunitha knew she was willing to defer her own marriage for a few years. She did not want him to tell her that it was over between them and that he was marrying someone else. Marriage was not to feature in her life for the next few years. She knew that he would probably not wait and it would be best to make a clean break. But not yet, she decided. She enjoyed him. The evening ended on a high note, as she had hoped.

* * *

On her return home, Sunitha went directly to the kitchen. Here, she had another large slice of pineapple. She had never been regular, but this was the first time her period was this late. She was not pleased. 'Shit!' she said aloud. *This better bring it on or I'll be in real trouble*, she thought to herself. She drank her can of beer and made her way to her bedroom, looking forward to a good night's rest.

It had been a long Saturday. Zaitun's absence had upset her. She had told Kumar about Zaitun but he was uninterested. Now lying on her bed, awaiting sleep to descend on her, Sunitha hoped she would receive news about her possible future studies in the next few days. The other thing she really wanted was for her period to come.

* * *

The week went by in its usual hurried pace. Kumar had called and asked if she would be having dinner on Friday as they had been doing the last few months. She saw no reason not to, and said 'yes'. On her return home, she found a letter on the dining table. Her mother had left it there, realizing that Sunitha had not noticed it earlier in the day. She quickly tore open the envelope and read the letter. 'Yes,' she said aloud. I think I've just been saved, she thought.

Once in her room, Sunitha took out a file marked MBA. She placed the letter on a pile of correspondence. She'd write her reply the next day. *Tomorrow will be action day*, she decided. She would start by informing her parents. They knew she wanted to move on and had not objected. *I will miss them*, she thought. *Thank God Rajan is just an hour away. At least they'll have one of us nearby*, she consoled herself.

Sunitha's thoughts shifted to her three close friends. *The girls will not understand when I tell them.* They will finally come around when they realize there's no turning back on my part. *They'll probably go on with the Saturday teas,* she thought. Sunitha had spoken to Zaitun on Wednesday. She had asked Zaitun how things were with her and Mazlan. Zaitun had been evasive. The D-issue seemed to have dissolved into the background for the time being. Sunitha wondered when Mazlan would threaten Zaitun with divorce again. But that was Zaitun's business. It was her prerogative to say as little as she wanted. Sunitha told Zaitun that they had missed her and hoped that she would turn up this week. Zaitun assured her that she would be there.

Sunitha spent the next few days writing all the required official letters. She felt no sadness resigning from a job that gave her so little pleasure. It had served its purpose. *Three more months of this and I will be in another world. A place I really want to be in,* she thought happily. On Friday she told Kumar her plans. He took this as the reason for her declining his proposal. He wished her well. She was pleased with his response. She knew that he was now lost to her. She felt no regret.

* * *

Sunitha's drive to Vasantha's house was a long one. It was raining and there was a massive traffic jam. Sunitha made a mental note of things she had to do. She had to find a buyer for her car. That was her only financial asset. She finally arrived in Subang Jaya after a forty-five-minute crawl from Angkasapuri. Zaitun's car was parked outside the house.

Sunitha made her way into Vasantha's house after greeting Vas' ever-smiling maid.

Her three friends were seated at the dining table. Sunitha happily placed the walnut-cake she had bought on the dining table. Seeing the packaging, Malar quickly commented, 'Went to *La Manila* again, ah?'

'Yes! I decided to treat you all. I'm celebrating today.'

'You said yes to Dr Kumar?' Vasantha teased.

'Tun, these two have nothing else to talk about. Marriage. Marriage. Marriage.' Sunitha purposely attempted to draw Zaitun into the conversation. Zaitun managed a smile. Sunitha settled for that.

'So, what's the good news?' Malar asked.

'I've got a place at the London School of Economics. I've accepted the offer.'

Malar and Vasantha didn't look impressed. There was silence at the table. Zaitun broke the awkwardness, 'Better drink your tea, it's getting cold.'

'You're not going to take our advice after all,' Malar started.

'You're giving up Dr Kumar for another degree. You're a silly woman, Sunitha,' Vasantha continued.

Zaitun came back to rescue Sunitha yet again. 'We should be happy for Sunitha. She's doing what she wants. She can get married later, if she wants.'

'Tun! Don't take her side. You're supposed to tell her she's making a big mistake,' Vasantha said with exasperation.

'Yes, Tun. If Sunitha says no to this good match after going out with Dr Kumar for so long, no Indian mother is going to allow her son to marry Sunitha,' Malar added.

Sunitha was surprised by Zaitun's support. She had expected Zaitun to support the two women, or to say nothing. She liked what Zaitun had said. Sunitha wondered how much she really knew Zaitun. She had always been with them. They had grown up together and somehow remained friends through school and adulthood. Yet she knew so little of Zaitun's thoughts.

'Hei, hei, listen. Okay, Kumar proposed marriage two weeks ago. He clearly likes me. I don't know if we actually love each. We have never said the four-letter word to each other.'

'Love. You need more than that for a marriage to work, my dear.'

'Sunitha, he's rich and he's educated. Don't throw this opportunity away. You may live to regret it,' Malar joined in.

'I've already declined Kumar's proposal. I've told him about my plans to continue my studies. He has accepted my decision and so must you,' Sunitha said in a matter-of-fact manner. 'Oh, come on, please be happy for me. I'm going to be leaving in three months. Forget marriage for me for a while. We'll talk about marriage when I return.'

Vasantha made a face at Sunitha. That's a good sign, Sunitha decided. Malar gave her a playful pinch. 'Hope that hurts. It's to let you know that I disapprove.'

Zaitun placed a saucer with a piece of cake in front of each of them. They ate quietly.

* * *

The next two weeks went by quickly. Everything was falling into place bar one. Sunitha had gone into her second month without her period. She hoped it was because of all the excitement in her life. She was generally accustomed to irregular periods. Then one day she awoke feeling generally unwell. This went on for a few days. The days started poorly but as school drew to a close, she usually felt slightly better. Alarm bells began to ring.

No, I can't be, she told herself. *I'll wait another two days and then I go to the pharmacy and buy a kit,* she decided. *Damn Kumar and his bloody coitus interruptus.* The risks were supposed to be minimal. *What bloody luck if I am pregnant.*

Sunitha had put on her best performance on Saturday, to make sure the three women suspected nothing. She cancelled dinner with Kumar. On her way home, Sunitha bought the required kit.

In the kitchen, Sunitha found a small bottle. Taking a deep breath, she took it and walked into her bedroom. I do not need a baby. Zaitun and a host of other women do. 'This pregnancy will *interruptus* my studies, *interruptus* my life, *interruptus* everything. Damn, this might just be the *coitus interruptus* of my life!' Sunitha said to herself.

She opened the package and placed the strip of paper on her table.

'It's up to me now.'

The Dastardly Twin

Venus, take my votive glass;
Since I am not what I was,
What from this day I shall be,
Venus let me never see.

—*The Lady Who Offers Her Looking-Glass
to Venus*
Matthew Prior, translated from the
Greek Anthology (1718)

'It's death, isn't it?' she queried, in her casual way.

'Death's not the adversary. I would gladly welcome it,' he replied. 'You don't understand. Death is the end of things. It is living that matters. I want to be alive. Do things I did fifteen years ago. Feel the way I felt then. I don't want to slip into a quiet existence.'

She looked intently at him. She didn't know if she should feel sorry or be amused by him. *Why the obsession with being young?* she wondered.

'I'm growing old too! And I quite like it. In fact, I'm looking forward to a quiet life. No more running around. I want to slow down. I want to sit back and sip life like wine.'

He could not help but stare at her as the words flowed out of her mouth. Almost disgusted, he replied, 'I don't like wine and I don't want to sip my life. I'm used to mouthfuls, like beer, and I don't want to settle for less. You go ahead and get ready for grand-motherhood.'

His violent response surprised her. She wanted to tell him that he was wrong, but she changed her mind. She couldn't help thinking that the men had finally arrived! *So, this is what happens to the modern, ageing bachelor.* He had begun to sound just like some of the old, single women she knew. But even they didn't seem as paranoid to her.

'I expected you to understand! It is not a matter of being forty-five. It is the process of reaching there. Nobody is going to ask me how old I am. They are going see my face, my hair, my hands and they are going to say, see how he's aged? He was once so good-looking.'

'But, Paul, you still look good. You are still doing the things you did ten years ago. So why all the worry? We all grow old. It is inevitable. It's allowing it to happen gracefully that matters. With age, there comes a different kind of beauty.'

Only ugly people say such things, he thought to himself.

She had lost him. He looked distracted like he was in another world. Something in the glass had caught his attention. She wondered if he was trying to see his reflection. She knew he was vain, but this was ridiculous. She felt like he was stretching his fears a bit too far.

'You've not listened to a word I've said,' she complained.

He apologized, pretending not to have heard her. He wondered what beauty there could be in ageing. He called for the bill. He paid and they rose to leave. They bid each other farewell and parted. He hailed a taxi and was soon on his way home.

The streets were crowded with people. His eyes kept looking at the older people. He didn't want to be like them. They walked slowly. He thought he saw despair in their eyes. Some were bent, some were walking with sticks and some were holding on to others for help. No, he didn't want to grow old like them. He closed his eyes, but their images remained. They haunted him.

The taxi stopped in front of his apartment block. He decided to walk up the three flights of stairs to his apartment. 'I could do with the exercise,' he told himself. The apartment looked the same. Everything was in its proper place. Nothing seemed to have changed since he had bought it five years ago. There was hardly any wear and tear. He envied it. It seemed to him as if the apartment mocked him. *Everything will probably be just like this even after I'm dead*, he thought with some bitterness.

Death was not the problem. Why people worried about it, he wondered. He wanted his death to come swiftly and if God willing, quite painlessly. Death ends things. 'I can handle Death,' he told himself. He recalled what his friend had said earlier. He felt like she was losing her sight and also her sense of beauty with age. No one looks better with age. Only a fool would fall for that compliment, he thought. And God forbid that I grow old. The very word itself gave him a feeling of distaste.

He walked into the bathroom. He removed his contact lenses and gently washed his face with the facial cleanser that had promised a wrinkle-free face. He peered into the large mirror in front of him. Mechanically he wiped his face with a toner and then applied his moisturizer. Lines had begun to form on what was once a smooth complexion. He had outwitted pimples, but all those creams and lotions had merely delayed the inevitable.

No, they aren't laughter lines, he sighed. *Another fool had told me that*, he recalled.

He hated evenings. He hated looking at the tired face in the mirror at the end of each day. He hated the offending grey hair that had to be plucked. Soon he would have to resort to other means to hide the grey hair that seemed like invasive force on his scalp. It was not just the face. The skin on his hands had begun to slack and to his utter disgust, even his trim stomach had began to show signs of a slight bulge. The proud designer beard had been swiftly removed should anyone see any of the offending grey strays in it.

At seventeen he had wanted to be twenty-one. And at twenty-five he had wished time would stand still for him. But he went on to become thirty-five and older. It was worse than rowing against the tide. It was like travelling in an open sea, not knowing the final destination, and having no control to stop or to turn back.

The face in the mirror was a stranger he would rather not meet. But every time he looked at it, the stranger was there. Even as he applied his night cream, the stranger mocked him and all his attempts to shake him off. Yet, it did not deter him. He knew the minute he stopped his struggle he would be even more desolate. Placing the final jar in the cabinet, he walked out of the room that had begun to feel like his personal hell.

He was ready for bed. He remembered Keats, *My spirit is too weak—mortality weighs heavily on me like unwilling sleep.* The restoring sleep he sought after each night never came. He rose each new morning only feeling more desperate. As he was about to switch off the table lamp, he caught sight of a photograph. It was a handsome young man. Standing erect and proud. It seemed to be from an age ago. Like youth, time flies. *I was happy then,* he thought.

Darkness enveloped the room as he switched off the last lamp. He lay still on the bed. It did not matter that he returned each night to a lonely bed. It did not matter that when he died, he would not leave anyone after him. It did not matter that he was once young.

What did matter was that he was once young and now old. What did matter was that he would never be young again. What did matter was that women would no longer give him hungry looks. What did matter was that other men would no longer be envious of him.

'Let me die before I get old,' he whispered his nightly one-line prayer.

As sleep slowly overtook him, he slipped into another world. There was a party going on. There was a good-looking young man dancing with a strikingly beautiful young lady. Heads were turning looking at them. He recognized the young man. It was him. He could not make out the girl. It did not matter. He was strong and vibrant. The music was loud, and the room was thick with cigarette smoke.

The beat of the music grew faster and soon, there were only a few couples on the dance floor. They were intoxicated by the rhythm. Suddenly, it was just him and his partner on the dance floor. The others had stopped dancing and were clapping to the rhythm. All eyes were on them. The music ended and he stopped, exhausted.

Even in his dream he could feel both the physical tiredness and the emotional rush he used to experience at the end of an exciting dance. Needing to refresh himself, he went to the restroom. He looked in the mirror. There appeared a beautiful figure next to his. It startled him. The face broke into a smile, which was then followed by a sneer. Then, loud laughter rang out. 'Don't you know me?' he asked. But before he could say anything, the figure answered, 'I'm Death,' still laughing at him.

It has come to claim me, he thought.

'I've not come to claim you. I've planned something crueller. You're going to live! For a long, long time!' Death screamed joyously. 'Indeed, you don't fear me, so I have given you to my twin brother, Decay,' it howled and disappeared. He moved restlessly on his bed.

Morning soon broke. He awoke feeling even more tired than the night before. The dream was still vivid in his mind. *I must have had a vision*, he thought.

And as he rose from his bed he was greeted by a wilting flower in a vase. He did not remember putting it there.

He sighed as he moved towards the vase. He picked up the decaying flower and without giving it a second look, threw it in to a wastepaper basket. It struck him that he could knew what flower it was. 'It was a beautiful sunflower. It was once beautiful, but is now fit for the bin,' he said to himself.

Suddenly, he said aloud, 'God, let me die before I grow old.' Feeling drained of all energy, he just sat on the bed.

Husband Material

Ravimama, my mother's youngest brother, was seated across the table, looking intently at me. The last time I had met him was four years ago. I have no lack of Mamas. My mother has six younger brothers, but he was my special uncle. The last time I had met him was when he visited us to wish me luck as I was about to leave for my university studies in Kuala Lumpur.

My parents were ecstatic when I got a place at the university. So was I. I was finally leaving the close-knit Indian community in Buntong. My mother had decided to use Ravimama as a point of reference for university studies.

'Ravi, you were in UM. Please advise Shanti. She's still a child and doesn't know anything about studying in a university,' my mother said.

I was not embarrassed. I was still a child in their eyes. My uncle looked at me mischievously. Taking me by my hand, he said, 'Shanti, come let's go for a drive. I have to pick Uncle Anand up from his flat. We are off to Pulau Tioman for a holiday. We can talk while I drive.'

He had hardly driven five minutes when he stopped at a Kentucky Fried Chicken restaurant. We ordered a drink each. He looked at me and asked, 'So what do you want to know about varsity life?'

I looked at him blank-faced. Sensing my discomfort, he started, 'It's a different kind of life, on campus. I cannot really prepare you for it.' I was relieved that it was not going to be a lecture. He could have done this at home, I thought. Then he started. And that was when I wished the earth would open and swallow me up.

'Shanti, like I said, it is a different world. Study hard but do have a good time. This is your only chance to be away from home. Remember, you're responsible for yourself and your studies,' he began.

'Your mother will be preparing for your wedding by the time you graduate. So, if you're ever going to find a husband on your own, this is your opportunity,' he said and looked straight into my eyes. I thanked all the gods on our family altar for giving me a dark complexion. Here was my thirty-one-year-old bachelor uncle giving me advice about marriage when he had chosen a single life. My face did not betray my thoughts.

'Do you know about contraception?' he inquired. I nodded. 'I'm not suggesting you have sex but if you decide to, then for your own sake, take precautions. Remember, you're the one who gets pregnant, not the Krishna who was lovey-dovey with you,' he continued. 'Don't forget you can catch VD or herpes, not forgetting HIV infection.' I felt the whole restaurant could hear him.

I started fidgeting. He held my hands gently. 'Shanti, I don't want to embarrass you. You are a big girl now. And an attractive girl, too. There'll be lots of men out there who would want to go out with you. Choose who you want. But remember, you come from Buntong. The Indian community does not take kindly to modern girls. Worse still, it has no place for pregnant girls, even if they get an honours in Economics.'

I thought he had finished but I was wrong. 'I have just a little more to say. Bear with me. You may even thank your Mama one day. If you don't eventually find yourself someone you want to marry while you're at the university, there is little chance you will once you start working. By then, your mother will have contacted all the relatives, and your photograph will have been placed in the marriage circuit. So, try to find a good man, someone who meets your tastes. It would be helpful for your case if he's doing a professional degree and comes from the same background as us,' he concluded.

I stared at him, my mouth agape. He smiled and asked me if I had any questions. I shook my head and wondered what my mother would do if she knew what Ravimama had just said. He was honest. He had said everything as a matter of fact. I liked that. I don't think any of my other uncles could have said it quite the same way.

'Thank you, Ravimama,' I said. And before he could say anything else, I asked why he had not married.

He looked at me and a slight smile broke on his face, then it faded just as quickly. His eyes took on a sad hue and he said, 'I'll tell you if you ask me again, after you graduate. You're not ready for my story yet. Who knows, we could even compare notes.' He smiled again and the sadness disappeared.

We finished our drinks and left for Uncle Anand's flat. We arrived quickly and Ravimama ran up to his friend's flat. They returned in a short while, with Ravimama carrying Uncle Anand's bag. I was promptly sent to the back seat.

I did not know it then, but that was the last time I was to see Ravimama all throughout my varsity days.

* * *

'Ravimama, I'm not sure how much you approve of me. I did try to follow your advice. There was enough information on safe sex to scare me about being promiscuous. Anyway, I did not go to bed with the first available man. I imagined every Indian on campus was somehow related to us or would know some member of the family.'

I could tell Ravimama was not prepared to hear this from me. I wondered if he would stop me right there and then, and was grateful when he remained silent and allowed me to continue my story.

'First year was fun. I met lots of guys, but nothing really happened. It was great going to the movies and parties, especially with no curfew hours. It was when I returned to campus after the long vac that I met Indran. We were in the same late-evening tutorial group. I had seen him before, but he kept to himself. It rained heavily one evening and he offered to share his umbrella. It was raining too heavily to walk to the bus-stop, so I accepted his invitation for teh-tarik at the cafeteria.

'We talked about courses and living in PJ. He was from Kuantan and was sharing an apartment with three other guys. I was impressed. I was sharing a house with six girls. The rain eased and we did not have any reason to stay so we left.

'The next time he spoke to me was a fortnight later. We crossed paths almost daily and exchanged smiles. He invited me to a movie. I told him that I was waiting for a friend to confirm about her party. He gave me his telephone number and asked me to let him know. The party was on, but I told Indran it wasn't. Now, I can't even remember what movie we saw. This was my first date with him! After the show, we stopped at some hawker stalls and ate *Hokkien mee* and drank Chinese tea. He hailed a taxi, and I was at the front door of my house by eleven-thirty.

'Indran did not ask me out for a while. It did not bother me as I was busy with my friends. He popped into my life again with an invitation to a play that was being staged on campus by a foreign drama troupe. I accepted and even volunteered to pay for my ticket. He quickly declined my offer.

'We watched five actors playing the various characters in *A Midsummer's Night Dream*. It was entertaining and we both had a good time. After the play, we walked around the lake on campus. As you know, it is not a big lake. He gently touched my hand, and I moved my fingers into his. We strolled, hardly speaking. Lost in our own thoughts about each other.

'We walked down the road and Indran stopped the first taxi that passed. Just before he dropped me off, he asked if I would like to have lunch with him the next day. I agreed.

'Well, Ravimama, this was the beginning of the romance of my campus days. Your words remained in my thoughts. Indran was a gentleman and he obviously had money. He just fell short of one of your requirements. He was not doing a professional degree. The family will just have to cope with that.

'We began seeing each other daily and I thought myself forward-thinking and went on the Pill. We spent more and more time in his apartment as he did not have a roommate. It was about three months later that we went to bed.

'We were lying on the bed and kissing. He gently broke from our embrace and asked, "Shanti, shall we make love?" It was all so romantic. There wasn't a tinge of illicitness in his request. I didn't want to say no. I didn't say yes too eagerly either.'

'You don't look surprised, Ravimama. I'm glad. I thought I knew what I was doing. Yes, I was willing to lose my virginity for this man who I had grown to trust and love. I gathered that night that Indran was no virgin. He was gentle and loving. It was pleasurable and I knew I wanted more of this kind of loving.

'You know, Appa and Amma knew I was going out with a guy and Amma threw hints about not giving myself to any man. She even said something about people not buying the cow when they could get the milk free. I invited Indran to Buntong during the long vac, but he declined. I did not push him.

'When we returned for the final term, Indran informed me that his parents had found a girl for him, and he was to be engaged soon. An anger I never thought myself capable of rose from within me. I screamed, ranted, and cried. He sat on his bed and just looked at me.

'I finally quietened down.' He continued. 'I have no say. My parents dropped two bombshells on me,' he said softly. 'My father informed that my future in-laws have been paying for all my studies and expenses for the last four years. Marriage to their daughter is the only form of repayment,' he said.

I stood there feeling sorry for myself. He moved towards me and held me close. His heartbeat was racing and I bit into his shoulders. We slumped onto the bed. I must have fallen asleep in his arms that evening. I woke up with a start. The room was dark and Indran was asleep next to me. Lying awake, I moved closer to him and inhaled his scent, wondering how much longer this would go on.

Morning finally broke, and as I got out of bed, he too awoke. I told him I was going home. He called a taxi for me. I went to my room, packed a bag, and returned to Buntong.

Amma was surprised to see me back mid-week. I told her I was free and wanted to spend some time at home. She looked worried but did not ask any questions. Appa knocked on my bedroom door just before dinner and came into the room.

'Shanti, is everything alright?' he asked, seating himself on the chair next to my bed. 'It's not like you to come home without even calling us.'

'I know, Appa, but I'm okay. Nothing to worry about.'

'You don't look okay. You can talk to us.'

'There's nothing to say. I just wanted to rest.'

He dropped the subject and asked me to come downstairs for dinner. Walking behind him into the dining room, I asked Appa where you were. It was only then that I found out you were in Sabah. That you and Uncle Anand had set up some small business in Kota Kinabalu.

Amma was still in the process of getting the food to the dining table. I scooped rice onto the plates, and we sat down to eat. Amma and Appa talked about their day while I wondered what Indran was doing.

On the third day he called. I was glad to hear his voice.

'Hi, Shanti. Why did you run away?' he asked.

'I came home,' I replied.

There was silence for a while. He spoke again, 'Please come back. I didn't want to do this to us.'

I wanted to feel sorry for him. But I was the one who was being dumped. I could not feel sorry for him.

'Not yet,' I replied and put down the phone.

Two days later I was back on campus. Indran found me in the cafeteria where we usually had our lunch. He held my hands and asked if I would like to go back to his apartment. I agreed. Once there, he held me in his arms. I did not tell him that I did not want to leave him. We made love and fell asleep. We woke up, made love, and fell asleep again. I didn't want to lose him. It was me he loved.

'Ravimama, I wish I could have left him then. But I couldn't. He told me that he was to be engaged to this girl at the end of the month, but he wanted to be with me. I didn't think him selfish, as I wanted him, too.

'After the engagement, my weekends were miserable. He was away in Kuantan with his family and fiancee. I returned to my books. I got my Second Class Upper but lost my lover. As the term drew to a close, we grew more frenzied in our love. I did not go home. I continued to rent the room in PJ. Told Amma and Appa that I would be getting a job in KL. Indran, too, kept his room. He was also trying to get a job in KL.

'We were together as often as we could, remaining in KL, using job-hunting as our excuse. Just before graduation, I got a job as a reporter for *Malaysian Business*. I still work there. Indran wasn't so lucky. No, actually, I wasn't so lucky. He didn't get any job offers. But his future in-laws wanted to have the wedding soon anyway.

'Well, Ravimama, I was on the way to becoming an adulteress. I didn't feel like one. I'm not sure how an adulteress feels. Guess, I didn't feel guilty. I assumed that we would continue seeing each other like before, although I knew things would change.

'Amma and Appa complained that they hardly saw me, of course. But I used my work as an excuse. They surprised me with a new car as my graduation present. It dug into their savings, and I was grateful to them. They knew I was still going out with my varsity boy-friend. Amma's hints that I should get married grew less and less subtle. One day, she called and informed me that there had been a proposal for me.

'"Shanti, Malar Aunty called. She said there's a lawyer working in KL who's interested in you." She paused, waiting for me to react. When I didn't, she continued. "He's twenty-six and a nice boy. He even owns a house."

'I told her I wasn't thinking of marrying. She reminded me that it wasn't going to get easier to find a good catch as I grew older. "There are many Indian girls who are graduates and unmarried," she reminded me. Then she added, "I'm not asking you to agree to marry him. Just agree to go out with him for dinner and see if you like him."

'I told Amma I'd call her if I decided to meet him. I didn't. A few days later, I received a letter from Appa asking me to think about my future and meet the man they thought was good husband material. Appa did ask if I was still going out with the boy whom I knew during my varsity days.

'Ravimama, the boy whom I knew during my varsity days was getting married, but he still wanted me. I accepted the arrangement. A few days before the wedding, I discovered this, too, would have to be altered. Indran informed me that as he still hadn't found a job, his father-in-law had suggested that he do his MBA in America; his wife would go with him, of course.

'I didn't go to his wedding. We met in his PJ apartment when he returned from his honeymoon. Sorting out his belongings was his excuse. We had two days together. That was the last time I was to be with him, for now. He left for America six days ago. He called me on Thursday. God, I miss him.

'I rang home yesterday and Amma told me you were in KL. She said you and Uncle Anand were here for some business meeting. Amma said you'd be staying at Plaza Hotel. Thought I'd try my luck and call you. I really wanted to talk to you. Thanks for seeing me.'

Ravimama smiled and drank his beer. I was not sure what his thoughts were. He looked at me and held my hand. 'Mama, I have just gone on about myself. It's been your turn to listen. The last time we met I was the listener. I've not quite finished my story, Ravimama. But I want to know something first. You said you'd answer my question, about why you didn't marry, after I graduated.'

He looked into my eyes and said, 'I did, in my own way.' Then I understood. I wouldn't have four years ago. He was right. I told him I was happy for him. At that moment, I wished Uncle Anand was there with us.

'You don't have to feel sad for me, Ravimama. Of course, things are not all right, but when are they?' I tried to sound philosophical. I smiled at him lovingly, and he smiled at me in return. 'Ravimama, I'm not ecstatic with the way things are. But I'm not going to allow Amma and Appa find me a nice boy. I don't know how things will go between Indran and me. I'm in no hurry to find out. For now, I've a career and I still love Indran. But I may even meet another man. I'll leave my options open,' I managed to say. I was beginning to feel slightly weary of myself.

'I'm suddenly feeling hungry. Let me take you and Uncle Anand for dinner,' I suggested.

At the mention of Uncle Anand's name, Ravimama grew quiet. I sensed a sadness I had not noticed before. I had shared all that I had gone through and yet I hardly knew anything about my uncle's private life. My parents never broached the topic either.

Ravimama cleared his throat and before I could ask, he continued, quietly and finally, 'I'm afraid it's going to be just you and me tonight. Uncle Anand is having dinner with his parents. His mother has found another nice Indian girl she wants to marry him off to.'

The Desired One

As he entered his lover from behind, the beloved cried out '*Avven*', howled, turned around and bit deep into his neck. The loving embrace turned violent. Blood spurted out from the neck and he convulsed so violently that it broke the light body beneath him. A terror-struck spirit looked on from a distance. His earlier efforts to do good had all gone awry. The God of the Dead had his day. When their bodies were found, they were still locked in an embrace, one with the head of a dog.

* * *

It was a time of lockdown and social distancing. Everyone was staying indoors and neighbours who had generally been strangers now kept their distance even more. Kannan and Nandan shared a two-room flat in one of the less affluent Kuala Lumpur suburbs. It had a mixed group of residents: Malaysians, migrant workers and some of dubious origins. The two men kept to themselves and had no friends among the flat dwellers. It was mostly a head-nodding casual relationship when they saw each other in the lifts or corridors. They kept everyone at a safe distance; not too friendly a smile, and the fewer questions the better. Now with everyone wearing masks, Kannan and Nandan could not actually recognize most of them anyway.

Kannan drew closer to the sleeping Nandan. They were still facing each other. Nandan had dozed off mid-sentence as he often did. Kannan gently laid his lips on Nandan's. He pressed a little harder. Nandan moved closer and his lips gently parted. Kannan, encouraged, gently pushed his tongue between his lover's parting lips. He felt Nandan's hand draw him closer into an embrace. In the warmth of their pressing bodies, they slipped into an undisturbed slumber.

When Nandan awoke towards the morning, he watched Kannan's gentle breathing. The snores of the night seemed to have subsided. Over the last three years they had become immune to each other's snoring. His throat was dry, and he felt a sore throat coming on. His body felt slightly warm and was aching. He got some water and decided to take two Panadols. Nandan began to panic, thinking of all the symptoms of the dreaded disease spreading across the world. He had been careful about following all the guidelines.

As usual, last Monday, he had met Mark and got him the week's groceries. Mark had seen him through his university days and Nandan was happy to be of help to him. Mark was elderly and not very mobile after a stroke, but seemed to be in general good health otherwise. They had spent time chatting and worrying about how things were going. Mark's dog, Ben, sat by his master as they spoke. Neither wore masks as they felt they were in their own private space. Later, as Nandan got up to leave, he hugged Mark and asked him to take care and be safe. Nandan remembered what he and Kannan had done together the night before. He hoped he had not picked up anything from Kannan. Or he had not picked up the virus at his workplace. It had been safe, and no positive cases had been reported in the places they had visited.

Around 7 a.m., Nandan began to panic. His body ached more. He wasn't sure if he was just imagining it. Kannan was still asleep. Nandan called Mark. The phone went to voicemail. Nandan waited a few minutes and called again. Voicemail. Now Nandan was feeling ill and guilty. Nandan called Mark again. This was the fifth call that went to voicemail.

Kannan walked into the hall at ten in the morning. 'Thought we were going to have a Sunday lie-in,' he said.

'I was thirsty and then couldn't get back to sleep. Thought it better that at least you had a good rest.'

'Ready for some *roti canai*?'

'I'll make coffee. Can't wait till lunch?'

'Think I worked up an appetite after our workout last night. I need food.'

'You *tapau* for us, lah. I'm suddenly tired and don't feel like leaving the flat.'

'Lazy bugger. I get the food first then shower when I get back.'

Kannan left with his mask on. Nandan was feeling unwell. The Panadol did not help. His body hurt and his breathing was laboured. It had been a while since he'd had an asthmatic episode. He went to the drawer and took out his Ventolin inhaler. He took three puffs. He had been constantly hearing about the symptoms and he couldn't tell if what he was experiencing was the real thing. He called Mark again.

This time there was nothing on the other end of the line. No voice message even.

Nandan did not know Mark's family or friends. Nandan had met Mark at a charity event Nandan had organized with his Form Six schoolmates. He had caught Mark's attention. Nandan struck Mark as intelligent. Mark was rich and wanted to help young deserving Indians. They kept in touch and when Nandan applied to a local university, Mark helped pay his fees. Mark supported Nandan from a distance, making no impositions. When Mark suffered a stroke a year later, his movements were impaired and Nandan began to visit him more regularly. Soon it became a weekly routine, one where he helped with the dhobi and grocery shopping.

Kannan was taking an unusually long time. It should not take this long to pack roti canai and return. *Must be a long queue. Social distancing, MySejahtera, taking temperature*, he thought to himself.

Kannan appeared almost an hour later. 'The bloody Mamak was closed. A worker tested positive. They are sanitizing the place. I had to walk a bit before I found a coffee shop. I got two packets of *nasi lemak* instead. That was the fastest and there was no queue for it.'

Nandan sat opposite him. He was beginning to panic. He didn't want to say anything and hoped he would feel better soon. He drank plain water and gargled with salt water. He hoped that would help. It did not.

'I'll go catch up on the sleep I lost this morning.'

'You want to go to bed at midday?'

'I'm feeling warmish. I've taken a couple of Panadols. My old asthma seems to be acting up. I used the inhaler. Let me sleep it off.'

Kannan did not think much about it. They had been together most of the week. He had forgotten Nandan's weekly visit to Mark's earlier in the week. Kannan knew of Mark's kindness to Nandan. He liked it that Nandan was caring towards Mark. 'Hey! Gratitude is a virtue. Send my regards to your Mark Mama,' he had said to Nandan that Monday.

Nandan tossed and turned, trying to sleep. He was feeling more and more uncomfortable. Finally, he was worn out and fell asleep. Kannan checked on him around 2 p.m. It was an odd Sunday. But then again, in the last two months everything had changed so drastically; today was not so unusual. Kannan got tired of playing games on his computer and watching sports on Astro. The daily statistics soon appeared on the news. This virus was not going away.

Nandan woke up and made his way to the hall. He did not look as if he'd had any rest. He looked unwell. Kannan began to worry and took Nandan's temperature. It was 40 degrees Celsius. Nandan got up to get some water and fell to the floor. Kannan carried him to the sofa. Nandan was lying unconscious as Kannan called 999. Within an hour, three men in full PPE gear came and took Nandan away. They wrote down Kannan's mobile number and said that they would keep him informed. They asked him to do a test the next morning.

He tested negative and was asked to stay home for the next ten days.

Kannan never got to speak to Nandan again. Four days later, an unlisted landline number rang Kannan's mobile phone. *Not another sales pitch*, he thought. 'Hello, Mr. Kannan?' a soft-spoken female came on the line. On hearing his confirmation, she introduced herself as Sister Kwan, a staff nurse from the COVID ICU ward. 'I'm sorry to inform you that Mr. Nandan Balasubramaniam passed away. He died a few hours ago. His family has been informed. We are letting you know because you had called the ambulance, and we have your contact details. I'm sorry for your loss.'

'Is there any way . . . I can say my goodbyes to him?'

'No, sorry. It's strictly family.'

I'm his family, he wanted to say. *I've been his family for years,* he wanted to add. 'I understand,' he replied. Kannan looked at the empty side of their bed.

'I called you because in his delirium, he called out your name. He said, "I will come back", those were his final words,' the staff nurse said.

'Oh, Nandan!' Kannan lay on Nandan's pillow and wept. Kannan wept for his friend and lover. The last few years were bearable for both because they had each other. It was almost midnight when he awoke. The pillow which was often drenched with their sweat was now soaked with his tears.

Kannan prayed. 'Please come back to me. In any form you choose, come back and love me again. I cannot live without you. Show me a sign and I will find you. Dear God, please let me find him.'

Alsa, a good-natured but bumbling spirit, heard Kannan's plea. 'Here's my chance to make amends,' he said to himself. Alsa took pity on Kannan. He granted Kannan's wish.

* * *

A dog stood forlorn and lost in a house. His master had gone away unexpectedly, taken away by strangers. He feared those men whose faces and bodies were fully covered. Ben had hidden under his master's bed. Once they left, he came out and lay on his spot on his master's bed.

Soon, the food his master had laid out for him ran out. He now drank water from the pails in the bathroom. As the night drew on, Ben lay on his master's bed. He missed Mark. He whimpered quietly and occasionally howled. In the dog's heart, he made a wish: *Give me a companion like Mark who will love me. I don't want to be left all alone.*

Alsa heard Ben's plea. In these days when people were dropping dead like flies and many hearts were being broken, he felt sorry for this creature, and granted Ben's wish.

* * *

A few miles away, a broken-hearted young man yearned for his dead partner. Alsa, seeing these two sufferers, used his powers to grant their wishes. They would all find each other as the desired one. This was the third and final wish he granted. Nandan's distressed face flashed in Alsa's mind as he recalled granting Nandan's dying wish.

Alsa vanished, having bestowed the three wishes required of him at his first level of spirit internship.

* * *

Ben felt a little peculiar when he woke up on his master's bed. He felt stretched and naked. In an unfamiliar fashion, he stood up. Saw his reflection in the mirror opposite. There stood a tall and handsome young man looking back at him. He heard a voice. Ben looked around. There was no one.

'Ben, it's me. Nandan, your master Mark's friend. I'm not sure what happened. We are in this body together.'

Ben let out a yelp that only Nandan heard.

Ben was familiar with Nandan's voice. It was a kind voice. Ben started to whimper. Nandan was confused and Ben's whimpering didn't help him. Nandan said to Ben, 'Don't worry, I'm with you. We will figure this out.' Ben slowly calmed down. There was an eerie silence. Two minds both lost in thought. It was unclear to Nandan how they could co-exist. He remembered he wanted to live. Now he was alive.

Nandan remembered his human body had died and he had desperately wanted to come back to Kannan. He just could not work out how Ben had a human body that they were both sharing. It was mind-boggling. He felt glad to be alive. He remembered Kannan. He wanted to go back to him. That certainly posed a problem now. They were in Mark's bedroom. The voice in his head was screaming: How did he and Ben get into this human body? He did not think Ben had transformed into a human. And where was Mark? He could sense Ben's presence. And he was glad he didn't feel anything really doggish. They were in a human body together. Nandan was mostly in control. Ben tried to be calm in an unfamiliar body. Nandan sensed Ben's occasional whimpers. Nandan thought Ben was missing Mark or was confused. *I'm confused*, Nandan thought. Nandan remembered not being able to get in touch with Mark. It dawned on him that Mark had probably passed the virus to him and was dead.

Nandan found Mark's clothes that were two sizes bigger than his own. A belt solved the pants issue. They were about the same height. He would go with a baggy look until he figured out what to do. Nandan began to think of some practical matters. *How will I explain my presence in Mark's house and Ben's disappearance?* Having looked after Mark the last few years, he knew where the supplementary debit card was. He had used it to buy the weekly groceries and sometimes get cash at the ATM for Mark.

Nandan felt a hunger. He wasn't sure whose hunger it was. He wanted biscuits. He knew that was Ben. He decided he would have a meal and both of them would have their hunger sated.

At the ATM he withdrew 3,000 Ringgit—the maximum that can be drawn in a single day, Mark had told him. He felt a guilty pang; he was taking Mark's money for himself. He quickly left. *The security cameras would have recorded my transaction but how would they trace me?* he briefly worried. *No more 'illegal' and risky activities,* he decided.

Nandan and Ben had a mild Indian meal. Nandan wasn't sure how Ben would react to it. He also bought cream crackers, just to be on the safe side. Ben seemed quiet. *I'll watch what I eat and drink. Will have to give chocolates a miss.* Nandan made sure he didn't look suspicious. *How do I now make sense of this before I talk to anyone, especially Kannan? It's too early to go and sit in a park.* He decided to go to a café he had never been to. *I have to sort this out before I go anywhere near Kannan.* He ordered fresh apple juice and a slice of butter sponge cake. *Safe options.* Nandan was so preoccupied with his own thoughts that he did not sense any agitation Ben was feeling.

Nandan decided to gather his courage and call Kannan. His voice choked when he heard Kannan's voice: 'Hello . . . Hello . . . Hello?'

Nandan replied, 'Hello, I'm sorry to disturb you. I'm a friend of Nandan's. My condolences to you. I'm sorry to disturb you. I'm trying to contact his friend Mark and there's no answer on his phone.'

'Mark died three days ago at GHKL.'

'Oh God!' Nandan replied.

Kannan thought the voice suddenly sounded familiar. 'Who is this?'

'I'm Mark's former colleague. Thank you.' Nandan put down the payphone before Kannan could ask another question. 'Kannan, sweet baby,' Nandan said to himself. Ben was quiet. Mark's silence began to make sense.

Nandan returned to Mark's house. He could sense an excitement in Ben. When they were in the house, Ben quieted down. Mark was not in his regular chair in the living room. Mark's living siblings were abroad and certainly would not be back over the next few days. Nandan knew where to find their contact details but wasn't going to contact them. Nandan's mind was racing. He had quite forgotten about Ben till he heard some sounds. *It will be okay, Ben. Don't worry. You are with me. I will take care of you. We won't be seeing Mark. I will be with you from now on.*

'All-right,' Ben replied.

'Did you just say "all right", Ben?' Nandan asked incredulously.

'Yes, I can talk,' Ben replied.

Nandan needed to sit down. There was a talking dog with him in another man's body.

'It's not another man's body, Nandan. I woke up this morning and I had changed into a man. *You* are in *my* body.'

'Thank God you didn't change into Kafka's monstrous insect,' Nandan laughed almost hysterically. This was the first time he had laughed in a while and soon he broke down. The reincarnation and body-snatching were too much for him. He dozed off in the living room. Ben remained awake, watchful.

When Nandan awoke, Ben said he needed to pee. Nandan decided to sit on the toilet bowl to avoid anything untoward, not having done this before with a dog in him—or him in a dog, as Ben thought.

The rest of the day, Nandan talked through his plans with Ben. Nandan did all the planning. It was all very new to Ben, who grew restless; this was not his idea of being a man's best friend.

* * *

Over the next two days, Nandan went back to his neighbourhood. He watched Kannan from a distance. Kannan returned home at the usual time after work. Unlike before, he was alone. Nandan ached to be with his grieving partner. Ben was silent, sensing Nandan's emotions. Ben remembered sitting at Mark's feet. He yearned for his master's comforting voice and the treats Mark gave him.

Nandan bought the cheapest mobile phone he could find. He got a prepaid account. He remembered that Kannan and he had an account on Grindr they still used to chat with other gay men. He hoped Kannan would see his message and that way, he could find out Kannan's state of mind.

Nandan called his profile Nanben21, which was close to the Tamil word 'nanban' which means 'friend'. He did not want to freak out Kannan with a profile name like 'Nanban' which was too close to his own name. Nandan sent a condolence message to Kannan. Said he had heard of Nandan's passing from a university mate. He asked Kannan if there were any prayer sessions he could attend, with lockdown SOPs of course.

The next day, Kannan replied thanking him for his message and informed him that Nandan's family was not doing any prayers during these pandemic days. Nandan thought of the next plan of action. He decided the direct approach would be best. A face-to-face meeting at a convenient place. Nanben21 asked Kannan if they could meet for coffee. Nandan was a long-time friend he had lost contact with, and he wanted to meet Kannan just to catch up to talk about Nandan. He gave his mobile number and signed off as Ben. After he pressed SEND, he wondered why he had used Ben's name.

Kannan read the message on Grindr. He had not spoken to anyone about Nandan's passing. Nandan's death weighed heavily on him. Here was someone who knew Nandan and would not judge them. He thought about it and the next afternoon, he texted a message inviting Ben to a café near his flat. He added, 'Please send a photo so I can recognize you.' Kannan thought this would deter any imposter. Kannan and Nandan's photo was already on their Grindr profile.

The thought of seeing Kannan again set his heart racing. Ben seemed to make no demands of him. Ben had heard Nandan's thoughts, and this made Ben miss Mark even more. Nandan thought he heard a howl. He wasn't sure, as Ben had spoken to him earlier. Nandan tried to be attentive towards Ben. Nandan was grateful that Ben was not difficult. That a man and a dog could occupy a single body, he didn't think it possible. He imagined he had a sleeping dog within him. Ben sensed Nandan's thoughts rather unhappily.

Nandan had less than twenty-four hours to decide how he would reveal himself to Kannan. His main worry: How do you tell your grieving husband that you have returned in another man's body with a dog in tow?

The café was quite empty. Nandan did the necessary MySejahtera registration and found a table at the furthest end. Nandan, true to his nature, had arrived early. He sat strategically looking at the entrance. He saw a familiar face approaching. Nandan's smile was hidden under his mask. Ben made no sound. Kannan saw him and nodded. It had been nearly two weeks since Nandan had come so close to Kannan. He feared his voice would choke. Ben whimpered, Nandan moved in his seat. He stood up. For the first time in years, he was shaking Kannan's hand. The hand which already knew every part of him.

'Hi, Kannan.'

'Hey, Ben.'

'Thank you for meeting me. I wanted to see how you were doing.'

'Managing.'

Nandan's eyes welled with tears. Kannan was a little surprised.

'This is a horrible time. So many deaths,' Nandan said.

Kannan thought he heard the same voice that had called him a few days after Nandan's death. A waitress interrupted them and took their orders.

'Kannan, when you received the news of Nandan's death, did the person say anything to you?'

'Why?'

Nandan hoped the hospital had informed Kannan of his dying words. 'I was wondering what he might have said before he died.'

'The nurse who called me said . . . Nandan mentioned my name and said he will come back to me. She said he was probably in delirium.'

'What did you say when you heard of his death, Kannan?'

'I was heartbroken. I cried. I cried and prayed. I begged God to send him back to me. I begged God to send Nandan to me in any form. I wanted him back so badly.'

'Kannan. *Avven* . . . *Avven, naan terippi vandrikaren, Avven,* I have come back to you, just as you prayed. I have kept my promise to you.'

Kannan stared at the man sitting before him. The only person who ever called him *Avven* was Nandan. He only called out *Avven* during their most intimate moments. No one else knew this but Nandan.

Nandan's excitement grew on seeing Kannan's recognition. Ben moved uncomfortably in their body. Ben had always been a carefree dog, roaming as he pleased in Mark's house. Being in a restrictive human body, with no control over his own mind, his own limbs, was far from what he had been accustomed to. He was trapped.

As Nandan willed their body to reach out and hold Kannan's hand, Ben felt Nandan's intense yearning for Kannan. It was at that same moment that, unbeknownst to Nandan, Ben's own instinct to survive was beginning to overwhelm him. All Ben needed was time and the perfect opportunity—he would be free again.

Callas and a Piece of Blue Cloth

Robert greeted each morning with the newspaper in hand—going through the classifieds and the obituaries more specifically—a habit he had inherited from his mother. As a child he used to watch her, morning after morning, reading obituaries, making sure she did not miss the announcement of any of her friends' passing away (that's what she called it). Mother was dead now, of course. Robert was not sure how much longer this ritual would continue, not that he was in his death throes himself, though some of his friends were. Robert had been diagnosed HIV-positive five years ago, but he did not feel any less healthy. *There are still some of us fifty-seven-year-old queens around*, he told himself.

Then his nephew called from the university.

'Hi, Robert, I'm afraid I've got some bad news,' Steve announced. Robert was surprised to receive a call from the nephew who lived with him, and was completely unprepared for any bad news. Before he could ask what the news was, Steve continued. 'I just found out that Suresh died last Tuesday.'

'Oh . . .'

'Robert? You still there?'

'. . . thanks for letting me know,' was all Robert managed and replaced the handset on the phone.

Robert didn't have the it-took-some-time-for-it-to-sink-in feeling. *How typical of Suresh,* he thought. *Even to the very end.* Robert was not sure if he should be angry, bitter or sad. Things had not turned out the way he wanted. He hoped they had for Suresh. *So, I didn't get to see him off even,* Robert thought to himself, half-swearing at Suresh's family for not putting an announcement in the newspapers.

The news of Suresh's death weighed heavily on Robert's mind. He had to lie down. He made his way back upstairs to his bedroom. He felt slightly light-headed. Not dizzy, but kind of a floating feeling. Lying on his bed, he thought, *It's finally over, my love affair.* It was his love affair, alone, as Suresh had walked out of it more than thirty years ago.

Robert lay restlessly on the bed. He couldn't bear being alone. He rang Kevin and invited him over for tea. He was pleased with Kevin's immediate willingness. When Kevin arrived at five, Robert had showered and prepared a pot of tea and was ready for him.

'You didn't sound well. Are you all right?' Kevin enquired.

'I'm fine. I received some sad news, though.'

'Someone's died?' Kevin asked.

Robert nodded. 'Suresh.'

Kevin said nothing. He had been half-joking when he had asked the question. Now he was not sure what to do. Saying he was sorry suddenly seemed trivial.

'Steve told me this morning. It's been six days. Suresh must be quite cold in his grave now. I decided to give his wedding a miss, but I would have to wanted to say goodbye to him. Anyway, maybe it's better this way. I really don't know how I would have reacted if I had seen him again. But that is all over now. Suresh is dead and buried.'

Robert was silent. Kevin poured himself a cup of tea. He sipped it and waited for Robert to continue.

'What Suresh didn't know was that he did not take all of himself away from me. I have kept a part of him for the last thirty-six years. I stole a part of him and I could not tell him what I had done. Kevin, I didn't feel guilty about taking something from him then. I still don't.'

Kevin thought Robert was rambling but said nothing. Robert was a good friend and he was here for him.

'Mine's not a story of unrequited love, you know,' Robert resumed. He paused for a moment and an odd smile broke out on his face.

'God, not another faggotty love story by a despairing old queen, you may think . . . but I'm afraid it is about love, at least while it lasted. And yes, it is about an old queen but she's not despairing.

'Despair is such a lonely word. Love doesn't lead to despair. Not if it's true love. I still love Suresh. Don't get me wrong, when he left me, I didn't feel very loving towards him. He decided I was just a phase in his life. I didn't like being a phase. He decided it was time to get on with his life and do what men ought to do, get married, and have a family.'

* * *

'Suresh had decided to make a clean break, but I hadn't known. I knew I wouldn't be the first gay man with a married lover.

Marriage, I knew, did not stop many men from returning to their lovers. Suresh was not among the many.'

For a few moments, Robert grew quiet then suddenly, he said, 'Suresh loved listening to Maria Callas. "Do you feel the passion in her voice?" he would ask. He played the aria, 'Una voce poco fa' from *The Barber of Seville* over and over. Suresh was entranced by her voice. I would try to feel the emotions he wanted to share with me, but I just never got drawn into it. Quite honestly, I would have been quite happy sitting in the same room with him listening to Johnny Mathis.

'"You know," he'd say, "feel the emotions. Let yourself go. Don't let the words get in the way." Of course, I could never let myself go, not the way he could. I love words. I love their ability to say or not say. I love their ambiguity, double entendres and irony. Words are traps, though. We sometimes read things which are not quite there.'

'I have that opera somewhere in the CD rack. Shall I play Rossini for you?' Robert looked at Kevin, but before his friend could say anything, he continued as if he had forgotten his own question. 'Would I feel it now? I couldn't then. I was in love. My joy got in the way. Shouldn't I be able to feel it now? He is dead. And I have not felt joy for a long time.'

Kevin passed Robert another cup of tea. Robert took a couple of quick gulps and put his cup on the table.

'I really know nothing about opera,' Kevin confessed.

'Poor Kevin, I've bored you,' Robert replied.

'No, not at all,' Kevin said.

'You know, Kevin, I felt no bitterness towards Suresh. That probably saved me from despair. I did not become a reclusive celibate. Have you ever heard of any celibate homosexual? Anyway, I didn't become one.

'I learned fast, and from then on, I seldom mixed love and sex. When I got both at the same time, I reminded myself that it was a luxury and I mustn't get used to it.'

Kevin looked fondly at his friend. They had met about six years ago in a pub. It had been quite an innocent meeting for Kevin. Robert had made a pass at Kevin, who had not even realized that he was being cruised. Only when Robert became more forward did Kevin realize that the respectable-looking older man was gay and was trying to pick him up. Kevin had apologized profusely, as he thought that he had unconsciously seduced Robert. It was then Robert's turn to apologize. They both laughed away their awkwardness and went for dinner instead. That started their friendship.

Over the years, Robert had talked about Suresh to Kevin, and it was clear that Suresh had been special to him. Robert spoke of no other man although Kevin knew that he had been seeing others.

'Robert, let me take you out for a drink now,' Kevin suggested. It had been a tiring day for him at the office and after listening to Robert, Kevin really wanted a drink. 'It's Monday, and Gatsbys won't be too crowded.' Kevin wanted to joke about the bartender Robert had been eyeing.

To Kevin's surprise, Robert smiled and agreed quickly to the idea of going out. Kevin was right of course. The pub was not even half full. But then again, it was still early. They got their beers and found a table away from the loudspeakers.

'Are you going to tell me about this thing you took from Suresh?' Kevin asked, and almost immediately regretted mentioning Suresh's name.

Robert broke into another smile. This pleased Kevin. His regret dissolved. Kevin felt he must have hit the right note.

Encouraged by the change in Robert's spirit, he persisted. 'Come on then, you can tell me.'

'It's something terribly silly and romantic. I've not told a soul about it,' Robert began, then hesitated. 'You'll think me perverse.'

'Don't start yet. Let me get another drink. Same again?'

Robert remembered the day, the day he hadn't known then would be his last with Suresh. *He could have told me*, Robert thought. *Unless of course he himself didn't know.*

Kevin returned with their beers and caught Robert in a different mood. 'You all right?' Kevin asked, unsure if they should go on about what Robert was supposed to have done.

'Yeah, it's nothing,' Robert reassured his friend and took a mouthful of his beer.

Kevin watched Robert, not knowing what he was thinking or what he was about to tell him.

'Suresh and I were in Langkawi island for a long weekend. He had run out of T-shirts so I lent him one of mine. My favourite blue T-shirt which I was pleased to see on his body. He wore it a whole day under the blazing sun. We sweated profusely and, when he returned it, the T-shirt was saturated with him. I threw it into my own bag with my other clothes.

'Two days after we returned, Suresh told me that he had decided to marry a girl his parents had found for him. I wasn't actually surprised. I had always known that he would marry, and I hadn't thought that I was losing him. But then again, he didn't tell me he was leaving for good, either.

'The hurt came later when he refused to sleep with me. He said he didn't want to love me that way anymore. The next day, as I sorted my clothes for washing, I saw the blue T-shirt Suresh had worn. It lay with my other clothes that

I had taken on the Langkawi island trip. When I picked up the T-shirt he had used, a strong whiff of his sweat hit me. I brought it close to my face and inhaled deeply. It was all Suresh. I folded it and placed it unwashed in my wardrobe with my other T-shirts.

'During the early days of Suresh's marriage, I often took out the T-shirt and felt the presence of the lover I missed miserably. Soon I went out with other men and Suresh withdrew to some corner of my mind. Whenever he moved to the foreground, I would return to the T-shirt.

'For more than thirty years it's been my one constant companion. So, there you have it. That's what I took—some may call it a misdemeanour but for me it was an act of love. It was something I could hold on to and never lose. I have never felt like a thief and even now it sits on one of the shelves in my wardrobe.'

Robert finished his beer. Kevin looked at his friend and said nothing, not sure what to say. He picked up his glass and took another sip of his beer.

'Guess you really loved him,' was all Kevin eventually managed.

Robert smiled again.

* * *

Robert switched on the bedroom light. He yearned for the smell of Suresh's body. Over the years he had never ever wanted to wash the T-shirt. The smell seemed to have remained there for him and it often took him back to the Canaries.

Robert removed all his clothes and moved towards his wardrobe. He opened his wardrobe. The blue T-shirt lay in the middle of the pile of his other T-shirts where he'd put it back that very morning. Every time he had taken it out, he had folded it again neatly, making sure the armpits were unexposed. Anyone opening his wardrobe would have suspected nothing.

In ritual fashion, with his left hand he raised the T-shirts above the blue T-shirt, and he gently pulled it out with his right hand, then let the others drop. Robert went to his knees. He used both his hands and spread the T-shirt on his bed. He lowered his face onto the T-shirt and inhaled deeply into the armpits. 'Suresh,' he said softly to himself.

Tired by the day's events, Robert held the T-shirt in his hands and got into bed, quiet and naked. He switched off the light and lay with his beloved. Sleep overtook him quickly. Insomnia was never a problem. Tonight, he slept even more easily.

* * *

The sound of movement downstairs awoke him. It was already a quarter past nine. It being Tuesday again, Steve was cleaning the house. Robert's nephew helped with the laundry and cleaning of the house. This semester, Tuesday mornings were cleaning days as Steve had no lectures or tutorials.

Robert put on his dressing-gown and went downstairs. 'Good morning, Robert,' Steve greeted his uncle.

'Morning, Steve.'

'There's still some hot coffee in the pot,' Steve offered.

Robert nodded and poured the coffee Steve had left for him. Robert took his cup of coffee to the sitting room. He went to the CD rack and found the Rossini opera.

Steve went up to his uncle's bedroom and collected the laundry for the week's wash. He picked up the clothes on the floor and pulled off the bedsheet. He laid the bedsheet on the floor and threw the rest of his uncle's laundry onto it. As he squatted to make a bundle, he noticed another T-shirt on the floor. Steve picked it up and threw it in with the rest of the clothes.

Once in the kitchen, he placed the clothes in the washing machine and switched on the machine. Steve got himself a cup of coffee and joined his uncle in the sitting-room, where the music was playing.

'I heard Suresh died of a sudden heart attack,' Steve began. 'I met his niece at the university library yesterday. She said that you weren't at his funeral. Prema asked how you have been keeping. She assumed you were unwell.'

'Well, it's really all right. I think I'd like to remember him alive,' Robert replied.

* * *

Then the sound of Callas made Robert stop talking. Steve started to say something but Robert indicated to him to stop. They both listened till the aria ended. When it was over, Robert re-tracked it on his remote control.

'This was Suresh's favourite aria in the opera,' Robert told his nephew. 'He was really moved by whatever the singer was saying. He would ask me to listen and allow the music to speak to me. But it never worked for me. I really tried. I'm afraid I needed to know what the words meant. The music was not enough.'

'I think I know what she's saying,' Steve informed his uncle.

'Really . . . well, what is it?'

'Rosina wants an affair with a young guy she's just met called Lindoro. She's pretty determined and is going to defy her guardian's wishes so she can get her way—or something like that.'

Robert wondered if Suresh had ever understood the words of the aria. *How terribly ironic*, he thought, without any remorse. *She defied her guardian for a lover, and I was dropped for a marriage of convenience*. Still, Robert did not doubt Suresh's love. He just could not accept Suresh's terms after his marriage.

Steve heard the washing-machine stop. He left for the kitchen, leaving his uncle in the sitting-room, listening to the aria again. Robert sat alone and distracted. When the aria ended, he re-tracked it yet again. Steve returned from the kitchen with a piece of damp cloth in his hand.

'Robert, one of your T-shirts has got terribly torn in the washing-machine,' Steve announced.

The sight of Suresh's T-shirt torn and tattered in Steve's hand sent a deep searing pain in Robert's chest and radiated to his whole being. The lone tangible link to a treasured past, the only reminder of the love that had once illuminated his life—was irreversibly gone. But perhaps this was for the best. *With this*, he thought to himself, *I can finally move on*. He took another sip of his black coffee, the bitterness lingering on his tongue.

The Gift of Silence

Vasu was sitting reading in the living room. His younger brother Sunil was watching his favourite cartoon show, the *Archies*. They heard the sound of a car outside their house. Uncle Rama's car was being parked in their compound. It was another Thursday evening, and Uncle Rama had come to meet their father. As usual, Appu was seated in the front seat of his father's car. He turned to his father's seat just as Uncle Rama was getting out of the car. He remained seated in the car while his father went into Vasu's house.

Soon some neighbourhood children gathered next to where Appu was seated. They knew Appu. *Umai. Umai. Umai,* the children chanted. Appu sat uncomfortably in his father's car and looked out at the children. Vasu's mother came out of the house and scolded the children. Their fun was cut short. The tormentors always left once they heard Vasu's mother's loud yell at them, 'Leave the boy alone. How many times must I tell you?' Appu watched the scene before him. He probably still remembered what had happened some time ago. Vasu and Sunil had asked him to come out and play with them. The other children came and joined them, and suddenly Appu got agitated and made some loud guttural sounds and fled back into his father's car. He refused to come out of the car after that.

Today, after the other children had been shooed away by Vasu's mother, Vasu came out of the house and looked at Appu. This was not the first time he had found himself watching Appu. Appu did not look at Vasu. Vasu felt a little awkward staring at Appu. He wondered why he was looking at Appu as if he were a caged animal. He looked like just another boy. In fact, he was quite good-looking. He had a fair complexion, more pale than fair; probably he didn't go out in the sun much. Appu's hair was short and parted on the left side, making him look very much like a schoolboy. His eyelashes were long. Slightly too long for a boy. No smile on his face. He was looking at a book on his lap. *He isn't that different after all.*

Appu unfailingly accompanied his father every fortnight. His father came into their house, while he remained sitting in the car. The children continued to taunt him, and he stared back at them. Vasu never joined them in their chanting of '*Umai*'. He remained a by-stander. He knew he should have scolded the children, but he didn't.

One day, Vasu's mother surprised him. She suddenly asked, 'Vasu, why don't you speak to Appu?' Vasu looked at her rather confused.

'Amma, he is an Umai. He won't hear me, and he can't reply. I'm more afraid than anything just to be near him,' Vasu said.

'Afraid?' his mother laughed at Vasu. 'If you speak loud enough, he might be able to hear you. He understands simple English and hand gestures. He's not going to attack you,' she said.

Vasu thought about what his mother had said. *My fears are probably imagined about what Appu might do. Why did I think him of him as violent? He always sits placidly, holding an object or a book. My fears of Appu are unfounded.* The children had said if they touched him, they too would become like him. Of course, he didn't believe them.

One day, Vasu's mother asked him to try on an outfit she had sewn for him. They were rompers, a single piece of clothing, a smaller version of overalls. As he was trying them on, Sunil started laughing and shouted, 'Umai satteh! Mute person's clothes!' Immediately, Vasu took them off and told his mother, 'I don't want to wear that.' *All the children will be calling me Umai and teasing me just like Sunil. I'm not mute and I am not mute like Appu. I am not going to wear that Umai satteh.* He put the rompers on the sewing machine and walked away. He never saw them again.

* * *

The next time Vasu saw Appu was at the temple both their families worshipped in. Appu was in black track pants and a T-shirt. Vasu had finished his prayers and watched them from a distance. Appu walked close to his father and imitated what his father did. Appu and Uncle Rama started off their rituals with prayers in front of Lord Ganesha. They slowly went round and prayed to the deities outside the temple before stepping into the temple. They went and stood in front of the main deity. The priest came out with a tray of flowers.

Uncle Rama put his hands on the tray and signalled Appu to do the same. Appu put his hands on the tray. Vasu knew Uncle Rama was telling the priest Appu's name, *natchathiram* and *rasi*. The priest nodded his head and took the tray in. The priest chanted the mantras loudly. Vasu was quite sure Appu did not hear his name being mentioned by the priest. Vasu saw that his father had finished his conversation with another friend and was walking to their car where Sunil was waiting.

'You were watching Appu,' Sunil said accusingly.

'None of your business. Just get in the car.'

During the drive home Vasu was silent. Appu was on his mind again. *What was Appu's world like? How do you live in a world where you can hardly hear? Not being able to say a word. Not being able to hear music and songs?*

Each year as they both grew a little older, Vasu was aware of all the changes his body was going through. *Appu's body was growing too. Appu outgrew his rompers, and soon was wearing long track pants and T-shirts. It seemed odd that for one who barely moved much, Appu was wearing sportswear all day. All that Appu did and wore was for the convenience of the adults.* These thoughts about Appu bothered him, but he remained silent.

A few months later, Vasu's family moved to their new house in Bangsar and Appu's father stopped coming for his regular Thursday meetings with Vasu's father. Vasu and Sunil rarely saw Appu. They heard that he had started going to a special education boarding school in Penang. *How will he manage on his own? Maybe, he'll be better with others like him. Maybe he will now have a life of his own.*

* * *

A surprise overnight holiday trip to Port Dickson during Vasu's Form Three school holidays brought their two families together again. Vasu had thought less about Appu. He had become occupied with his school friends and was busy attending tuition classes for the public examination. When Vasu, Sunil, and his parents arrived at their hotel in Port Dickson, they were just in time for afternoon tea. It was a buffet. Appu, his younger sister, Rani, and parents were already seated at a large table with four empty chairs for them.

Vasu and Sunil greeted the elders and said their 'hellos' to Appu and his sister. Vasu sat at the chair next to Appu. Sunil gave Vasu a slight pinch. Vasu ignored Sunil. *This is awkward. What do I say to him? How will I say anything to him?* Vasu moved a little uncomfortably in his chair. If anyone had told him that this was going to be the start of a friendship between him and Appu, he would have laughed in their face. Sunil broke the uneasy feeling and said, 'Annan, let's go take some food. Look at all the cakes.'

Vasu looked at Appu and pointed at the buffet spread. To his surprise, Appu rose from his chair. His parents said nothing. Vasu was glad to see Appu get up and head towards the buffet. *This is new. This is a good development. I'm really pleased. He is just like us. What a difference over a few months.* The three of them took their food and returned to their table. Rani was lost in her book. Appu ate the food he had taken and got up to get some more. He looked at Vasu and nodded towards the buffet. *This was not the same boy seated in his father's car two years ago.* Vasu nodded and joined Appu, and they walked towards the buffet.

Vasu's father had mentioned that Appu was attending a special school. Appu looked very much the same to Vasu. Sitting next to him, Vasu could see Appu more clearly. *He's taller and slightly heavier. Way more confident. Looks cute too. His facial hair is beginning to grow. Has he begun shaving? Can he manage on his own? Silly me, he's mute, not disabled. Someone needs to tell him about his body odour.* Vasu continued feeling a little uncomfortable.

Appu took out a rectangular box from his backpack, which was beside his chair. He showed the box to Vasu. It was a draughts game box. It was an invitation to play. Uncle Rama looked pleased to see what was happening. Vasu decided to oblige. *I hope to god this game goes well. I've never played any game with Appu. If he gets angry or starts making loud odd sounds, like before, they'll say it's my fault.*

Appu was no push-over at draughts. Vasu had not played the game for a long time, and had never really been any good at it. *I am glad he didn't ask me to play chess. I suck big time at that.* They completed the first game quite quickly. Vasu lost the second game too. *This feels so different. I'm learning about Appu. I am feeling less able now. It's a welcome change from playing with noisy Sunil.* Appu looked at Vasu and touched Vasu's shoulder. It was the first time Appu had touched him. Vasu looked blankly at Appu, and then it dawned on him that Appu was saying thanks. Vasu smiled. He touched Appu's shoulder in reply. Vasu felt Appu's shoulders relax. *I'm communicating with him. We just did something together.* Vasu turned to look for Sunil. Sunil, however, had fled from the table in case he might get roped in to playing a game with Appu.

Both families retired to their rooms. Sunil came back sheepishly to their room a short while later. 'It wasn't so bad, playing draughts with Appu,' their mother commented.

Vasu nodded; he was lost in his thoughts: *It was a first. All my friends are pretty normal, at least on the surface. Appu has been treated like some kind of a freak and called names because he is different from us. Our parents taught us things, like respect. There was so much to learn on how to get along with someone like Appu. Why did I feel awkward with Appu? Was I feeling pity? Maybe I have just begun to see him as a person—*

'At least you won't have to ask him to shut up when you get irritated,' Sunil said.

'That's true. But how to hold a conversation with Appu?'

'Are you planning on becoming friends?'

'He's just another guy. He doesn't hear very well and can't talk. He's not an idiot.'

'Amma said that Appu was born that way. His parents consulted all the doctors. It's something to do with his brain,' said Sunil. Vasu was surprised Sunil knew so much about Appu.

'Such a shame. He's quite handsome and should be getting all the attention for his looks, and not the wrong kind of attention he's getting now.' Sunil lost interest in the conversation and walked away.

In the evening, the two families gathered in the lobby and made their way to the beach. 'A walk along the beach before dinner,' Uncle Rama announced. Appu followed behind his father, who was leading the way. They walked at quite a leisurely pace, wading through the water when the waves washed over their feet. Appu kept turning back and looking in Vasu's direction. *After all these years we have briefly connected after the failed attempt in front of our house a few years ago.* Vasu gestured moving the draught pieces with his hands and gave a thumbs-up sign to Appu, hoping he would understand what Vasu was saying, that Appu was good at draughts. Appu nodded. He then looked ahead, and continued walking behind his father.

It had been a long day, and everyone went back to their rooms immediately after dinner. Appu caught a chill and had a slight fever during the night. He stayed in their family room till everyone checked out of the hotel the next afternoon. As they were getting into their cars, Vasu walked up to Appu and touched his shoulder. Vasu waved and said loudly, 'Goodbye, Appu.' Appu managed a smile and nodded at Vasu. *My first word to Appu was goodbye, how odd is that.*

* * *

Vasu spent the next two years getting ready for his SPM examinations. He wanted to make sure he got the right grades to get in Form Six in a government school. The exorbitant fees for private education would mean the end of his schooling if he did not get a Grade 1. Appu was making good progress in his school too. He had started school a little late and would take a bit longer to do SPM for special education students. Vasu knew that Appu was intelligent, but felt that his silence held him back.

'We're having Uncle Rama and family over for dinner,' Vasu's mother told her sons one day.

'It's been a while since we saw them,' said Sunil. 'Hope you don't get challenged to another game of draughts,' Sunil teased Vasu.

'Ha! Ha!' Vasu glared at Sunil.

'You'll be surprised by how much Appu has changed,' said their mother. 'Going to that boarding school has given him confidence, and he tries to communicate with others.'

'Is he still mute, Amma?' Sunil asked.

'Of course, you dunggo. Sadly, Appu will always be that way. But he can now read and write in English and Malay. The teachers are very pleased with his progress.'

'I told you guys he is intelligent. He gave me a tough fight at that draughts game.'

'You just stink at it. Admit it,' Sunil teased his elder brother.

Uncle Rama and family arrived at 7 p.m. As Uncle Rama parked his car in their driveway, Vasu watched from his room as the car doors were opened. Appu was the last to open his door. Vasu looked intently at the youth who got out of the car. He looked just like any other tall teenager. Appu was dressed in a black collared T-shirt and a pair of slightly tight blue denim jeans. He turned and took out a backpack out of the car before he shut the door.

Uncle Rama's family was making their way to the living room when Vasu came downstairs to greet them. His mother had made sure there were enough chairs for everyone. Vasu made it a point to walk up to Appu, and held out his hand to shake in greeting. Appu took Vasu's hand and gave a warm handshake.

The adults began their conversation, and the young people were left looking at each other. The maid brought cordial drinks and that helped distract them from their discomfort. Appu opened his backpack. Sunil's eyes were filled with mischief and he wanted to ask if Vasu was ready for another game of draughts. To Sunil's disappointment, Appu took out what looked like a paperback novel and a small 555 notebook with a ballpen in the middle.

Vasu touched Appu's shoulder and pointed to the paperback, asking him if he could have a look. Appu watched Vasu. He then took out his notebook and wrote something in it. He then passed it to Vasu. Sunil came and stood next to his brother to see what Appu had written.

It read: 'I like Lat comics.'

Vasu opened the comic book. He saw a name neatly written on it: Dhaksina Ramathan. Appu pointed to the name and to himself. *That's his name. A lovely name and we call him Appu. I will call him by his name from now.*

And so began written conversation between the two boys. Vasu wrote in the notebook.

'What do they call you at school?'

'Dhakshina.'

'I will call you Dhakshina.'

'OK.'

After just a few exchanges in the 555 notebook, dinner was announced, and they made their way to the dining room. Vasu's mother had prepared an elaborate meal with mutton peratal, fried fish cutlet, chicken curry, and vegetables. Both the mothers made sure everyone got served. The adults continued with their conversation while the young people ate quietly. Appu's sister, Rani, was too shy to talk to Vasu or Sunil, and they didn't know how to engage in conversation with her. Appu was no longer treated differently. Vasu started seeing him like another teenager just like him and his brother. *I'll invite Appu to my room. I will start calling him Dhakshina. It should be like being with any of my other friends. I will learn how to communicate with him. I want to be his friend. There's something about him that draws me to him.*

'Dhakshina,' Vasu called out loud enough for Appu and everyone else to turn and look at Vasu. *Oops! That came out a little too loud. Need practice.* Vasu used his hand to indicate going upstairs. Dhakshina nodded his head in agreement and followed Vasu. It was quite clear that Uncle Rama was pleased with how the two boys were beginning to get along.

* * *

It was the long vacation for Vasu after his first year at university and Dhakshina was on a school term break. Over the last few years, Dhakshina and Vasu had kept in touch mostly through letters. They met up during weekends when they could. Dhakshina did not come back to KL unless there were some religious festivals his family wanted him to attend. Vasu made arrangements to pick Dhakshina and go out for the day. When Vasu called, Uncle Rama had no objections. The two boys had been out a few times before. He told Vasu that he would tell Appu and ask him to be ready by 10 a.m.

When people saw the two youths together, they saw nothing unusual about them. They looked like any other young men. Few noticed that one of them carried a small 555 notebook with him. They would pass the book back and forth between them and make various hand gestures to communicate.

The afternoon went by rather quickly. They played couple of games of ten-pin bowling at Shah's Bowling Alley, next to Shah's Motel in Petaling Jaya. They drove over to the A&W drive-in next door and stayed in the car as they ordered their meals. They planned what they would do after lunch in Dhakshina's notebook.

After they got their takeaway root beer Vasu drove to the nearby Taman Jaya park. They found a big tree and sat down under its shade. The lake in the middle of the park and a constant breeze made it bearable at that time of the afternoon. As they had done a few times before, they took out the novel they were reading. It had become a habit to read the same novel so that they could talk about it. Dhakshina showed Vasu the page he was on. Vasu indicated where he was. Vasu was slightly ahead of him. Dhakshina then wrote on the notebook, 'Too many things to do at school.' Vasu nodded. The broad tree trunk gave them ample space to sit against it and read.

Dhakshina put down his copy of *Watership Down* and started writing in his notebook, and a conversation began.

'Are u going to get bored with me? Want to meet some girls like the rabbits in WD?'

'Haha! No! I'm happy as we are. No, *doe* for me.'

'U sure?'

'Ya.'

Dhakshina was pleased with Vasu's replies, but thought it natural that Vasu might soon find new interests in the opposite sex like Vasu's other friends they had bumped into a few times while in Kuala Lumpur.

Vasu suggested they better leave before the office rush-hour traffic. As they got up, Dhakshina moved towards Vasu and gave him a tight hug. Vasu stayed in the unexpected embrace and said nothing. His feelings for Dhakshina he dared not utter. They drove back to Dhakshina's house in silence. Then waved goodbye to each other as Vasu drove back home.

* * *

Vasu looked forward to his meetings with Dhakshina. Reading books and sharing thoughts. Speech was soon replaced with gestures and writing cryptic messages. A few words were sufficient to get a message across. A private code emerged between them. They weren't secret messages, just a system the two of them had developed over the months and years. Together they used up quite a few 555 notebooks.

Their weekly letters often ran to several pages. Vasu's mother recognized the thick envelopes from Dhakshina. Sunil told his mum, 'Amma, just be glad they aren't hogging our house phone.' Their letters were quite a contrast from the messages they wrote to each other on the notebook. These were often merely functional. In their letters they shared their thoughts and future plans.

Dhakshina invited Vasu to Penang. Dhakshina had hardly got to see the island. School had kept him busy, and there were few outings. He also preferred his own company and had made few friends at his school. With a letter from his father, the school would give them permission to go out overnight. This they finally got to do. As soon as the school term holidays began, Vasu took a bus to Penang. They stayed at the YMCA hostel in Macalister Road. Being on a shoestring budget, it was preferable to staying in a cheap, sleazy, budget hotel. They did not mind the dormitory. It was a place to shower and sleep. They crammed in all the must-see tourist sights in their itinerary, and ended up in Little India often, for at least one meal a day.

Just before they were about to go to sleep on the second night, Dhakshina went over to Vasu's bed. Vasu sat up, surprised by Dhakshina sudden sitting on his bed with his notebook.

'I'm making wristbands from some coloured thread,' Dhakshina wrote.

'Wristbands?'

'Ya. For us.'

'Wristbands for us?'

'Yes. Rakhi festival in two months away.'

'Brothers tie them for sisters, la.'

'It can be for friends too. It is for protection.'

'We need protection?'

'Everyone needs protection.'

'OK. You make both. Ok?'

'Can.'

With that, Dhakshina returned to his bed. Vasu lay thinking about Dhakshina and his reason for both of them to tie bands round each other's wrists. *What brought that on? It is so sweet. Protection. I do want to protect Dhakshina. No, harm. It is not a thali. If anyone asks, I'll say we extended Rakhi between friends. Loving friends.*

The two days of running around trying to see temples and eating local delicacies left them both exhausted. Dhakshina pointed to the botanical gardens and Penang Hill on the tourist map.

Vasu wrote, 'Next time,' on the notebook.

'Next holidays,' Dhakshina replied below.

Vasu and Dhakshina took the last overnight bus back to KL. Vasu had organized the purchase of the tickets and they were seated next to each other. They were mostly asleep. Seated so close to Dhakshina on a long drive Vasu remembered his first thoughts about Dhakshina's body odour. These days they both smelled of Old Spice.

When they arrived at Puduraya Bus Station in KL, Dhakshina's father met them. He gave a broad smile and led them to his car.

'How's Penang food, Vasu?'

'Excellent, Uncle Rama.'

Dhakshina smiled as Vasu gestured eating and drinking. Dhakshina sat next to his father. Vasu sat at the back, exhausted, and wanting to get to his bed.

* * *

Jaws was the blockbuster movie everyone was talking about. Vasu made arrangements with Dhakshina's father for them to watch the movie. Vasu arrived early at the cinema and bought their tickets.

He stood outside the cinema waiting for Dhakshina to arrive. Standing across the road he watched Dhakshina get off the bus. The pedestrian light was green and people were already crossing the road. Dhakshina saw Vasu waving at him. Dhakshina walked behind a couple.

The pedestrian lights turned amber. He walked a little faster. The couple in front of him looked left on hearing a vehicle heading towards them. Dhakshina heard nothing. He saw them move faster before him. The next thing Vasu saw was Dhakshina being hit by a speeding motorcycle. Dhakshina was flung off his feet and he hit the tarmac with a loud thud. The motorcyclist and the bike fell a short distance away.

Dhakshina lay unmoving in a pool of blood. Vasu could hear himself scream as he ran towards Dhakshina. A crowd gathered round them. Dhakshina's body lay in an awkward twisted position. He did not move. Vasu held Dhakshina's hand. People started gathering around them. Vasu looked despondently at Dhakshina. An ambulance finally arrived with two men in white uniform. One checked Dhakshina and the other spoke to Vasu. Vasu looked blankly at the men in white uniform. Something within Vasu snapped. He just stared at Dhakshina's lifeless body.

The two men spoke in Malay. Dhakshina was barely breathing. There seemed little they could do. Dhakshina was placed on the stretcher and taken into the ambulance. Vasu followed them and got into the ambulance too. Dhakshina slipped away as Vasu held his hand. The ambulance staff told Vasu what he had already sensed. His tears flowed down his cheeks and his body convulsed in uncontrolled sobs. Still, he had not said a word.

When they arrived at the Emergency, Dhakshina's whole body was covered with a white sheet. A dark red spot spread where his head lay. The hospital staff tried talking to Vasu. He remained in a speechless state of shock. They found Dhakshina's father's contact number in Dhakshina's wallet and called him.

Dhakshina's father arrived at the Emergency and he found a dazed tearful Vasu sitting by himself. When Dhakshina's father asked Vasu what had happened, he sobbed uncontrollably and could not speak. Dhakshina's father went to the reception. When he heard the news, Vasu heard Dhakshina's father break down in loud cries. Vasu's father came in just in time to hold his weeping friend. They were told that Dhakshina had been moved to the mortuary. They needed to go there to identify Dhakshina's body.

Vasu's father went to Vasu. Before he could say anything, Vasu hugged his father and wept inconsolably. Vasu's father asked him to stay in his seat. The two men walked towards the corridor that led to the mortuary.

Vasu sat very still. He kept seeing Dhakshina's body hit the road and Dhakshina in a pool of blood. He had run out of tears. He wanted to go back home and leave the present behind. He suddenly felt fatigued and closed his eyes. Vasu moved between sleep and wakefulness. After what seemed like a long time, his father returned alone. He touched Vasu's shoulders and Vasu broke down again. His father didn't ask him anything and led him to their car. They drove home in silence. The silence was broken by Vasu's occasional soft crying and the sounds of his sobs.

When they arrived home, Vasu's mother and Sunil rushed to the car. Vasu's father had called them from the hospital.

His mother saw blood stains on Vasu's shirt. 'He's not injured,' Vasu's father said to his wife and Sunil. 'He's in shock. He's not saying anything.'

'I'll take Annan to his room,' Sunil said.

His parents wanted to ask him details but Vasu said nothing. For now, all they knew was what they had heard of the accident from the ambulance men. Vasu's father left for Dhakshina's parent's home. His mother stayed to look after Vasu. When she came up to Vasu's room, with a tumbler of water and mug of Milo, Vasu was in the shower. She waited.

'Amma, you go wait downstairs. Let me help Annan.'

His mother left reluctantly, thinking that was probably best for now. Her heart went out to Vasu, and she was in tears again thinking of Dhakshina. Vasu came into his room in his towel. Sunil passed him a T-shirt and a pair of shorts. Vasu put them on in silence.

'Annan, we are all worried. Please say something. You can cry, even. We know how close you are to Dhakshina.

Vasu looked at Sunil. He remained silent. Sunil hugged Vasu, who stood still and silent. 'Here's some water and Milo. Please drink something.' Vasu drank the water and went and lay on his bed.

Sunil sat on the chair at Vasu's study table. He thought hard about how to get his brother to speak. Vasu seemed to be dozing. Sunil went downstairs and sat with his mother. They looked at each other, and Sunil held his mother's hand. Vasu was back home with them, but he wasn't the brother who had left home that morning.

Sunil checked on Vasu every hour till 1 a.m. He then fell asleep in his own room. He left the door open just in case Vasu needed anything.

Vasu refused to come out of his room. Spoke to no one. He lay on his bed, where sleep eluded him. He no longer saw Dhakshina's crushed body. Dhakshina was sitting next to him. They were walking in a garden; they were wading on a beach; they were playing a game of Chinese checkers. Dhakshina would look at him and hug him. Dhakshina was sharing an apple. Vasu watched himself walk towards Dhakshina.

Vasu's mother asked him if he wanted to go to Dhakshina's funeral. Vasu nodded. They left in his father's car. Sunil gently pressed his brother's shoulder. Vasu cried quietly and wiped his tears. On seeing Vasu, Dhakshina's mother wept aloud calling his name, 'Your good friend, Dhakshina is dead,' she repeatedly cried out. She hugged him. Vasu sat next to her by Dhakshina's closed coffin. Vasu cried with her until his father drew him away and seated him in the funeral tent.

Once the funeral rites at home ended, the mourners headed to the crematorium. Vasu watched Dhakshina's father light the funeral pyre. One of the elder relatives placed a cloth over his head and quickly led Uncle Rama away without letting him turn around and see the lit pyre. He was taken to a waiting car, and he left the crematorium. Vasu watched as the flames began to consume Dhakshina. In those flames, Vasu saw Dhakshina looking at him. Dhakshina smiled. He heard a voice, 'Don't be sad. I love you'. His silent friend, Dhakshina, finally spoke to him. As Dhakshina was released from this world, Vasu remained in his silence. Only his tears spoke of his sorrow.

* * *

One afternoon, Uncle Rama arrived at Vasu's home after what seemed like a long time, though it was less than two months. Vasu was in his room. Vasu's mother was surprised by his unannounced appearance. Dhakshina's death still weighed heavily on all of them.

'Come in. Anything the matter?' Vasu's mother asked.

'We were arranging things in his room. The maid found two boxes. There are letters and some small 555 notebooks which belonged to Dhakshina. I think Vasu might want them. How is Vasu?'

'He stays in his room. He wears his headphones and listens to his Walkman. Still has not said a word.'

Vasu's mother looked at the two shoe boxes Uncle Rama was carrying.

'Would you like to go up to his room?'

'Yes, I want to say something to Vasu and give him these two boxes.'

Vasu heard a gentle knock on the door. 'Vasu, it's Uncle Rama. Can I come in?'

Vasu opened the door. He was in a pair of shorts and T-shirt. He looked gaunt and tired. Uncle Rama was shocked by how much Vasu had changed over the last two months. He put the boxes on the floor and hugged Vasu. Vasu was unmoving and still.

'Thambi, Vasu, why are you like this? Dhakshina would not want you to be like this. It is not your fault that he died that way. It was an accident. You always looked out for him. He loved you. He wouldn't want you to be like this,' Uncle Rama's voice began to break.

'We found two boxes full of your letters and his 555 notebooks. Dhakshina had kept them. I think he would want you to have them. I'll leave it on your table. Read the notebooks. I hope these memories of how happy you both were will bring you back to us.' Uncle Ramu hugged Vasu again and left the room. He closed the door behind him. He wiped his tears before going downstairs.

Vasu looked at the boxes. He remembered the 555 notebooks Dhakshina constantly carried with him. He continued staring at the boxes. A sigh rose from deep within him and died in his throat. Vasu opened a box. In it lay neatly arranged notebooks and envelopes with his handwriting on them. Dhakshina had put rubber bands around them in small bundles. Vasu ran his fingers over the letters and notebooks. Among the envelopes he saw two wrist bands in a plastic bag.

'Oh! Dhakshina!' Vasu cried out. He cried out Dhakshina's name again and again and sobbed loudly.

His mother heard Vasu weep, calling out Dhakshina's name repeatedly. She too wept but with a joy of hearing her son's voice again.

The Interloper

When I walked into the dining room, the two men I had been with the night before were having their morning coffee.

It was not quite what I had expected, having walked into the hall and then going into the bedroom the night before. My thoughts had been more on the men than the slightly dim surroundings.

In the morning light, the designer kitchen and every other designer object in the apartment belied the two rather simple-looking guys I had met at the pub the night before.

I was the only one wearing clothes from the previous evening and after the shower, my clothes felt a little grimy from the previous night's sweat.

This was not the first time I had found myself in such a situation, although smiling at two guys at the same time was not something I often do.

'Ready for your coffee?' the quieter of the two guys enquired.

'Would it be too much to ask for tea?'

'Tea it is then!'

'Wilson makes great tea.'

Okay, the quieter one is Wilson and the chattier must be Raj.

The thought did cross my mind whether he was really Raj. Just about every third gay Indian uses Raj as a nickname.

Sunday breakfast with two guys you had got along quite comfortably in the bedroom posed the challenge of seeing things a little more clearly in daylight.

Before I could complete the thought, Raj said they were going to their club and invited me along.

They must have had a good time, I thought to myself. It wouldn't be a bad way to pass the afternoon, I would have amicable company, good food and who knows what the afternoon had in store . . .

'That'd be nice,' I replied.

* * *

I was in office packing my bag when an SMS came through: 'Want a repeat of last Saturday night? Dinner first. :)'

My fingers replied: 'Yup'

Looked like my weekend was taken care of.

Soon the weekend dates were moving into a regular thing. Dinner with Wilson and Raj and a few in-crowd friends. The level of discretion got lower and the crowd grew wider. Then back to their home and unhurried, delicious sex.

These regular weekends became more a regular thing than I had imagined. It's not a complaint. But neither was it as I might have anticipated.

Dating a guy, I could deal with quite easily. Intimacy with two guys was a little tricky, even for me.

Caught up between work and a new-found intimacy which I had not given a label to, I had shut out the rest of my world, thinking that my goings-on were not noticed, invisible and all so very discreet. This self-absorbed mode I was getting accustomed to received a sudden jolt, like a sharp slap of awakening, when I was alone with one of our regular dinner companions.

'Don't you feel like an interloper?' Janice asked.

What interloper? I could not get my head around what she was saying. And trust a lesbian to ask the question!

'Surely, a one-to-one gay relationship is hard enough. Those two must have gone through quite a few rough patches,' she added.

'I think I am making it gel quite nicely,' I returned. It sounded more flippant than I had wanted it to.

But her remark set me thinking. *What had I gotten myself into? A friendship with benefits. I assumed all three were benefiting from this relationship. Or were we?*

I had no cause to think otherwise. I had grown comfortable with the congenial relationship. And had stopped looking for other partners.

* * *

A familiar tone on my mobile signalled an SMS from Raj and broke my reverie.

'Free for drinks?' It read.

'Time?'

'7.30.'

'Leo's?'

'Yup.'

An unscheduled catch-up. Intriguing. The rest of the day went by uneventfully. I found myself sitting at the bar waiting for the two to turn up.

Raj arrived. No sign of Wilson.

'Wilson coming in a bit?' I asked, thinking it odd that he wasn't with Raj.

'It's just the two of us,' he replied.

We ordered our drinks.

'I have something to tell you,' he began.

'Don't take it the wrong way. Wilson and I really like you.'

Something told me a 'but' or a 'however' was about to follow.

'It's just that Wilson and I have an understanding. We meet guys and if we like them, we hook up together. Like what we've been doing. We have our own six-month arrangement. It's our cut-off time before any emotional entanglements set in. We had a few rough times before we decided on this. Now, it is always six months.'

I could not believe what I was hearing. I thought I would never be shocked. I don't think I was shocked actually. My feelings had not quite reacted to what I was hearing.

'Prem, today's our 6-month.'

So, no goodbye sex even, I thought to myself. I wanted to laugh. I was glad of my years on the circuit, my naïveté had been lost rather early with a few scars to show for it.

'Wow! I didn't see that coming, man! You guys are so smooth,' I said. I wanted to add slutty and slimy. But, held back.

'Cheers, Prem. Thanks.' A quick hug and I was looking at the back of a man who had briefly been in my life.

My so-called interloping days were suddenly brought to an end.

That night I was back on the circuit again.

Beaten Twice

Jack realized that he was going to be slightly handicapped travelling in Europe. In Asia and Australia, his perfect English was more than sufficient to see him through touristy interactions and social conversations. He wished he had taken up Spanish when he'd had the opportunity. Spanish and certainly not French as he didn't want to find himself in a class of giggly girls swooning over the French teacher. Although many years later, he regretted it when he found out the teacher was gay.

He was about to land in Rome and felt apprehensive. Jack was even uncomfortable when someone greeted him with a *Bonjour* or *Ciao*. He wanted to make the right impression. A tourist who had enough money to travel and not one who was trying to join the masses of illegals in Europe. *Not speaking a foreign language did not mean that he was an ignoramus.*

He hoped the immigration officer could speak in English. The queue quickly shortened and there was just his friend, Darren, ahead of him, completely unaware of his anxiety. He wasn't going to tell his friend his little fears and become the butt of their jokes.

Jack found himself face to face with a woman officer. The whole encounter ended with an exchange of smiles and a nod. No need to pee in his pants even!

Now relieved, he joined the others heading to collect his luggage. *Darren can do the talking and I will just go along with them.*

The holiday had been planned for a long time, especially with the exorbitant prices and the Malaysian Ringgit being so shitty. He had saved for a year. Scrimping and scrounging in order to go to the eternal city. It was something he had always wanted to do. He was way too young to have a bucket list.

He had a few must-do things in Rome and the others he'd go easy on, agreeing to do what Darren had planned.

Darren could not understand why they had to have different rooms. Twin-sharing would have reduced their expenses quite a bit, Darren had argued. Eventually, they had compromised when they found that with the new Airbnb options, they could find a two-room accommodation at a better price even. The reviews were good and the host was friendly enough. The place was booked and paid for.

Darren had done all the correspondence and the paying. Now they were ringing the doorbell to the apartment they would be sharing for the next four nights. The host was business-like. She showed them around the place, gave them the keys and left. Jack was quite happy Darren did most of the talking. The host spoke in whatever English she could, and it was way better than Jack's Italian.

The long flight had both of them knackered. After they had the wifi sorted and had sent out the obligatory SMSes, they hit the bed. The summer heat was just like being home but without the air-conditioning. Jack shed his clothes and jumped into bed. Darren probably did likewise. But Jack was not interested in finding out. They had been friends since varsity days. They shared the impersonal and their private lives remained private and confidential. With their careers as their utmost priority, neither seemed to have an obvious social life.

Twelve hours passed rather swiftly and now they were looking at each other across the dining table.

The itinerary for the four days had been planned out. They were going to do all the touristy things together. The nights were generally blank as they had not found too many touristy things to do.

Just as well, as the heat wore them out and they both were quite happy to buy beer and snacks and stay home and rest. The first night they discovered that TV channels in Rome were all in Italian. 'Now there's a surprise,' Darren quipped sarcastically.

Over the years, Jack had come to the conclusion that Darren had to be in bed by ten. By 10.30 he'd be dead to the world. This suited Jack just fine. Thanks to various dating applications, Jack had managed to get himself a date.

The guy spoke English and ticked off every requirement on Jack's checklist, the size of his cock being one of the main priorities. Language was not going to stand in his way on this matter; something he had discovered rather early in life.

Jack's date turned up as scheduled at 11 p.m. He was quickly sneaked into Jack's room.

Jack Lee was in the arms of the Italian lover he had dreamed of. They spoke enough English to get over the initial pleasantries. As he felt his new-found lover enter him and do all that his heart desired, Jack could not help but agree with all the talk about Italian lovers.

Jack lay satiated on his single bed. His friend came out of the bathroom. And Jack thought it best to make some small talk before ridding himself of his one-night stand.

'So, were you born in Rome?'

'No, I came from the Ukraine five years ago. It's European Union, ya!'

Jack suddenly forgot the sex and realized that he had not had sex with an Italian man.

Shit! There goes the second night, he thought to himself.

The next few minutes went by so fast Jack could not remember how he got rid of his short-lived 'Italian' hunk.

The next morning Darren and Jack were at the dining table having an English breakfast in Rome.

The morning was to be spent going to the must-see touristy spots followed by a quieter afternoon sitting somewhere cool. Just then Jack asked Darren if they could visit a famous cemetery which was near a metro station. Jack convinced Darren that it was not like the Chinese cemeteries in Malaysia. He had seen it on the Internet and it actually looked like a huge manicured garden.

Previously Jack had not made too many sightseeing requests. Darren agreed to Jack's proposition after hearing him describe the cemetery. The only times he had been to a cemetery was during Ching Beng. He had always considered himself lucky for not having too many dead relatives. His only dead relatives were his fraternal grandparents whom he had never known.

Later that afternoon, they arrived at the cemetery after a short train drive. The cemetery lived up to his expectations.

It was indeed a cool place. Lots of trees. It almost looked like a park. Everything was orderly and even labelled. Clearly the locals didn't have to walk over tombs to get to their relatives.

Darren wondered why Jack had a cemetery fetish. He had not been told that Jack had promised a young admirer that he would take some photographs of tombstones which had interesting epitaphs for the lad's final-year project.

Darren found himself a comfortable place and sat on a bench. It was still early in the afternoon and the place did not feel creepy.

Jack looked at the tombstones and was taking his photographs. As long as there were words, and they seemed lengthy, he was pleased. Within a short while, Jack felt he had taken enough shots, even if he did not understand much of what he took.

Darren was seated where he had left him but busy with his mobile phone. Jack was glad that his friend was neither bored nor grumpy.

'I'm done. Ready to go or you've got acquainted with this place?'

'Very funny! Let's go and be with the living!'

Jack was pleased with himself and was glad he had got this request out of the way. They decided it was appropriate to go to the famous fountain and make their wishes like the other tourists.

Jack and Darren returned to the apartment and the first thing Jack did was to send all the epitaphs to his love interest. Darren was in his room napping before they went out to see the night lights at the Colosseum.

However, Jack felt a sudden discomfort. He realized that he had not yet taken a leak since the afternoon. He had gone to the loo, but there was hardly a trickle. He let it pass. He must have drunk at least a litre of mineral water and a pint of beer.

Darren awoke and they were off to the city again to have dinner by the Colosseum. TripAdvisor had recommended a few restaurants that were trustworthy. The wine and the meal were memorable and water helped quench their thirst.

Back in their apartment, Jack could hear Darren peeing rather loudly. Still he did not have any urge to go. He went to the toilet and thought he would give it another shot. Nothing. Just a drop or two. He wondered where all that water had gone.

Darren was already in his bed. Jack was glad he had not arranged for a night caller. He lay on his bed and tried to distract himself. Italian TV channels were of no use to him. There was absolutely no channel in English. At least not on this television. He lay in bed and began to feel uncomfortable. There was a discomfort around his groin area. He hoped his bladder won't act up in the middle of his holidays. The very thought of having to burn his air ticket and buy a new return ticket was much too hard to bear.

He continued to toss and turn on his bed, unable to sleep. Feeling uncomfortable between his legs, he sat up and picked up his mobile phone. He looked at the photos that he had taken.

Tomb after tomb after tombs. Epitaphs one after another.

A sudden chill ran down his spine.

'But I had asked politely for their permission before I took the photographs,' he remembered.

'Still, better delete all the photographs before I offend them more,' he decided.

He clicked on a whole lot of photos of the various tombs and pressed delete. He then went to his Whatsapp Messenger and deleted his photo messages to his young friend.

Jack felt a little better once he had done that. Soon that discomforted seem to go away. He lay in bed trying to sleep. He couldn't. He decided he'd give it another try. He walked in the toilet and pulled out his cock and tried to pee. There was a slight stream. A sense of relief came over him. Worn out by the heat and his adventure, Jack returned to bed and fell asleep.

The next morning, without thought he went to the toilet and passed a long stream of urine. Remembering what he had felt the day before, he sighed in relief.

Darren was at the breakfast table. Jack narrated his night's ordeal.

'Your mother didn't teach you to ask for permission before you do anything with the dead, ah?' Darren asked incredulously.

'I did ask for permission mah!

'Haiyah! You asked in English!! The dead are all Italians. Wrong language, lah!'

Road Trip

Four Indian guys, east-coast-virgins-of-sorts, decided to visit the two Malaysian states under the control of the only overtly Islamic political party in the country. My friends and I had been deferring our visit for the last decade or so. We did not fancy visiting Kelantan while it was governed by an Islamic party with its strict social restrictions and religious laws. Then, the most recent general elections results made it worse as Terengganu returned to the Islamic party rule and Kelantan remained entrenched in its control. Seeing no dramatic political change in the near future, and unable to resist the lure of their cuisine, we gave in, all aware that there was no free flow of alcohol in the two states. We kidded ourselves that we could survive an alcohol-free holiday.

Over the last decade the four of us had grown into a relaxed camaraderie. We were a bit of an odd lot. Samy, the youngest in his early thirties, Regu slightly older (never told us his exact age), David had just hit forty last year and I was the oldest, about to hit fifty and, the leader of the group. I guess working in the same company, though in different departments, and being active members of the company's social club, and, more importantly, being Indian, kept us together.

Yet, we were not all that similar. Samy was a vegetarian and homely, David was a divorcee and a father of a young son, and Regu was the sportsman, he played football for his department in the company's football competitions. He was also a gym freak and our computer-savvy guy. And I had become accustomed to living on my own. I moved away from my family home at a young age and did my obligatory visits to my only sister's house for Christmas and the occasional long weekend holiday. My parents had passed away over the last decade. My house often became the place for the four of us to watch movies and drink beer.

* * *

The much talked about road trip arrived on a Thursday morning. We had all taken a couple of days off from work for a long weekend getaway. With the help of the Agoda App, the hotel rooms were booked, and a very flexible itinerary had been drawn out. The first day would see us arrive at Kota Baru and then we would be on our way back southwards through Kuala Terengganu, Kuantan and back to Melaka.

While it was still dark, even before the sun had awakened from its rest, we were all wide-awake in our car heading eastwards towards Kuantan. We stayed away from the highway and took the kampung road. Traffic was light and there were few fellow travellers on the road. The single-lane kampung roads would at times double to allow for easy overtaking.

Still, it was quite a challenge for me, so used to city roads with dividers and traffic lights. Despite the signs to beware of cows we saw none along the way. It was mostly green foliage on both sides of the road.

As we passed a few kampungs, we heard the muezzin's first call for prayers for the day. Soon the street lights were replaced by the rising sun breaking through the thick morning clouds. The temperature rose and we wound up the car glass windows and switched on the air-conditioning. We didn't want to smell each other's odours too early in the trip.

We continued along kampungs nestled in small towns whose names I only hear once in four years as the election results are announced. I loved the rustic atmosphere, but our mobile phones showed weak internet connections and I had no desire to live in these vicinities.

The small food-stalls, all Malay-run, were beginning to open for business. Samy asked, 'Guess there is no chance of a Starbucks drive-through in this neck of the woods?'

Regu, amused, replied, 'Just be grateful if you can get good *kopi-tarik*.'

Our aim was to arrive in Kuantan before the morning traffic jam in the city. The only breaks we had were pee breaks, that too was difficult to keep in sync with petrol stations that popped up along the way. I was willing to wait it out after hearing reports on the state of the toilets. This made me remember the billboards on some petrol stations informing prospective customers that their toilets were clean. These days you hardly see any more of these welcoming signs. *Must be due to a shortage of foreign workers to do our dirty jobs*, I thought to myself.

* * *

The breakfast at Kuantan was a very regular fare. Samy complained that we had gone to the wrong Kopitiam and not to the one mentioned on TripAdvisor.

'It could only get better after that shop,' he consoled himself.

'I'll ask my contacts in KT and KB to give some recommendations,' Regu said.

'You have contacts in KT and KB?' Samy asked.

'You guys aren't my only friends, you know,' Regu replied.

We were back on the road again and still staying away from the highway. The sign to take the highway seemed to be popping up every few kilometres. 'They want our toll money rather badly,' David smirked.

Soon we were passing durian stalls along the country roads. Small make-shift stands with durian vendors emerged as we passed the kampungs. We made our first attempt at buying durians as we headed towards Dungun. All four of us were in the mood for the fruit. After we passed a few stalls, we picked one with lots of durians, arranged in small pyramid piles. Unknown to us, they were arranged according to types and prices.

We got out of the car, and immediately, we were self-conscious that we will be seen as tourists and male tourists at that! Easy prey to these experienced durian-sellers. The stall was managed by three women, not an uncommon sight in Terengganu where many of the businesses were run by them. They looked at us, four Indian men, in shorts and T-shirts. I didn't venture into what ran through their minds.

David, the most competent Malay-speaking among us, started the transaction. One of the makcik, said, '*Lapan ringgit satu kilo*. Eight Ringgit a kilo. We looked at each other. We had seen signs for five Ringgit a fruit along the way. There was a durian glut throughout the country and prices had really dipped.

David, exclaimed in Malay, 'It's expensive. Earlier we saw signs for fruits at much lower prices.'

'For that price, you need to go to the orchard and get them yourselves,' the makcik replied.

We knew the price she wanted was still cheaper than those in Melaka. She guaranteed that they were sweet, and that she would pick the best fruits for us.

Regu decided to throw in his bit, 'These are kampung durians. There are so many rumours about chemicals being used in the huge orchards. Seem a good choice.'

'That's probably in Thailand or China,' David replied.

We asked the makcik to choose a fruit for us. She picked one, shook it in her hands, and said it would be a good fruit.

We agreed to buy the fruit she had picked for us. She promptly opened the durian shell. Lovely, thick, beige-coloured pods lay within the shell.

We took one each. It felt like sweet custard and tasted quite divine. We were in durian heaven. She took a second fruit weighed it and went through her routine. We waited like expectant chicks for their mother to pass them the freshly-found fleshy worms—though we certainly did not want to see worms in our durians.

'Two durians are enough for us, for now', Regu informed her. 'We'll spread our durian-eating along the way. Kelantan awaits us,' he told us.

Regu asked her why shook the durian. 'To feel the pods move. If they move, they are ripe and won't stick to the shell,' she explained in Malay. We made a mental note of the tip from the makcik.

We broke into an easy conversation with the makcik. Her women workers looked on. She asked us where we were from and if were on holiday. 'Ya, *jalan jalan*,' we said. She added, 'jalan jalan, *cari makan*.' She didn't hear Regu say, 'jalan jalan, *cari kawan*.' We broke into giggles like silly schoolgirls.

Unfazed by our laughter, she added that she still goes to Klang to sell '*jamu*' to lorry drivers. The change in topic struck me as odd.

'Is she saying what I think she's saying', I asked Samy. He nodded.

She continued, '*Mereka kata pagi, ah! itu keras*'. The men said in the morning *that* was very hard.

We made no query about the other product she was also pedalling. She was probably hoping to sell some of that aphrodisiac to us. But we weren't wanting in that department. We just nodded our heads, paid her the 16 Ringgit and got into our car.

'Stop by on your way back,' she called out to us.

We replied, 'Ya,' waved and drove off.

'She probably thinks we are on a dirty weekend away from our wives,' Samy said.

More laughter in the car. Silence for a short distance. Then suddenly, an awful smell wafted through the car. Automatically, we wound down our windows and yelled, 'Who belched?' This was to be repeated for the rest of the journey till we stopped in KT for lunch.

* * *

'I need to pee,' I announced. Giving no thought to the state of the toilet in the next petrol station.

'Well-timed,' David said as we were about to pass a petrol station.

While they others stretched their legs, Samy looked for the next recommended restaurant on TripAdvisor.

'The best local Malay food seems to be in KB. Top on my friend's list for KT is actually a Peranakan restaurant,' Regu reported.

'Is your source reliable? Are there Nyoynas and Babas in KT?' David asked.

Regu nodded in response. 'Apparently, you can also buy beer in a supermarket in Chinatown,' he added. On hearing that, our eyes lit up. The day had grown hotter and quite humid.

We found ourselves in the middle of Kuala Terengganu Chinatown, called Kampung Cina. This time no one complained about the food though we had not expected Peranakan cuisine in KT. Malay food was put on hold till KB. We bought the beer after our meal. Not so taboo after all. But no chilled beer in the supermarket fridge shelves. Fortunately, the supermarket was air-conditioned. It stood to reason, to our beer-thirsty throats that the beer won't be warm.

'Still no sign of a Starbucks,' Samy lamented.

There were no sympathies from the others. Samy declined the not-so-chilled beer and took over the wheel. For now, we settled for a six-pack and drank it in the car.

* * *

It had been a long day, and we were getting a little weary of being on the road. Waze indicated another hour and thirty minutes. We were making good time taking turns to drive but it was certainly a long journey.

Kota Baru eventually came into sight. We were more than pleased to find our hotel next to the river. KB, like other state capitals, had its fair share of traffic jams and traffic lights. It was quite amazing, at the least for me, to see some large old wooden bungalows next to dull concrete shophouses. The ugly was devouring what must have once been beautiful. The town would at some stage lose all its old buildings, I feared.

After a brief rest in our hotel rooms we met at the lobby for an early dinner. A Grab car took us for some serious Kelantanese cuisine. Regu's friend's recommendation was all he said it would be. Yati's *Ayam Perchik* restaurant did not let us down. We also had the first taste of local *keropok*. We ate to our hearts' content.

'You know what will go well with this fabulous chicken?' David asked.

'Beer,' we all responded.

We decided to take a detour and went to Chinatown before heading to the hotel. The Grab driver dropped us off under an archway, named after Admiral Cheng Ho, heading into Kota Baru's Chinatown.

'Cheng Ho came to KB too?' I asked.

No one bothered to reply. My beer-thirsty friends had spotted something, and they could not believe their eyes. The longed-for beer was within sight. They saw the iconic tiger logo, announcing the lager beer, pasted on the glass at almost all the food stalls. We couldn't believe this was in KB.

The food stalls were buzzing with customers. Looks like the KB Chinese were all here, and we four Indians. Later, we spotted a few Indians in the food stalls. We clearly didn't look local. We were the only guys in shorts. Samy and Regu bought the beer we wanted for the night. These were really chilled cold beers unlike those from supermarket shelves in KT.

Amidst all the food stalls, we spotted a few durian stalls. Their prices were most unappealing compared to what we had seen along the kampung roads. Then we noticed the only durian stall with a bunting claiming organic durians were being sold.

'Organic durians? Really? Is it really possible to grow organic durians in our orchards?' Samy asked. 'Who are they kidding? And did you see the price? I'd just settle for a musang king durian for that price,' he added.

Samy said we should ask them if they really meet all the requirements to call it organic. 'Want to be quarrelsome with the locals, is it? Worse still, we might get whacked!' David said.

David was being street-wise and so we got another Grab and left for the hotel before the beer got warm. We seated ourselves outside the hotel. It was a cool evening with a very pleasant evening breeze. It wasn't clear who had set up tables and chairs along the riverside across a row double-storey shophouses. The four of us sat at one of the tables, drinking our beer. We were a contented lot after the very long drive.

The evening grew on and we were on our third beer can. Regu's phone gave off the same tone we had been hearing throughout this journey. He briefly looked at it, typed a message and re-joined our conversation.

'Why do you keep getting messages with that tone?' David asked. Samy and I looked on. Regu looked a little uneasy.

'Sorry, I'm being *kaypoh* and intrusive,' David apologized. We continued drinking our beer. The streetlights had come on a while ago. There was a cool breeze, and we were quite comfortable just sitting there drinking our beer.

Regu looked at us, he hadn't drunk his beer since David asked him about the repeated message tone.

'Hey, Regu. David was just curious, lah. We all have been wondering about the messages you keep getting. It's quite different from the WhatsApp notification sound we all have. And during this trip, guess we kept hearing quite a lot of it since we were together in the car.'

'Okay. I really don't know how you are going to take what I'm about to tell you. If I can't tell you, there's no one I'm going to be able to say this to.'

The light-hearted atmosphere suddenly slipped away and an unplanned serious moment emerged.

'Those are messages from a dating app. Actually, it's a gay dating app . . . So, now you know. I've just told you . . . I'm gay. I really wanted to tell you guys some time ago. It's been bugging me that there's a part of me you don't know. And somehow, here, in the middle of our holidays, and in of all places, in Kelantan, I'm coming out to you guys.'

That was quite a surprise. We had never suspected Regu of being gay. 'I'm glad you've told us, I'm fine with it.' I was the first to respond to Regu's unexpected announcement about his sexuality. David and Samy echoed what I had just said.

'We want you to be happy. Glad that's out in the open. We'll keep it to ourselves, of course,' Samy said.

I got up and gave Regu a hug. He looked like a nephew who was suddenly vulnerable and needed a hug. He gently hugged me back.

As if to ease the atmosphere, Regu added, 'No worries, I don't fancy any of you.' That comment relaxed a slightly odd moment and we broke into laughter. We weren't sure what we were supposed to do with this information.

'I guess there won't be any wedding presents to worry for you,' I said.

'Don't be too sure. If the right guy turns up, I'll certainly let you know. It will be payback time for all the presents I've been buying for your relatives.'

I was happy for Regu. The younger generation seems to be more accepting and willing to come out of the closet. A burden had been removed for Regu. I had been holding back from my close friends and still did not have the courage Regu had just shown. I felt that this was a secret I would carry to my grave. I hoped that Regu would have a happier life than me. These three friends had kept me occupied and happy even. I had not even thought of any of them in a sexual way.

Unlike Regu, I had never thought of a relationship, let alone casual sex, or meeting men through dating apps. My only companion had been Internet gay porn, which I accidentally discovered. From then, I didn't have to watch hetero-porn to look at the naked men. My thoughts were broken on hearing someone call my name.

'Hello? James, a penny for your thoughts.'

'Sorry, I think the fatigue is finally catching up with dear old me,' I replied.

'Old? You're not old at all. Lots of miles to go in that tank of yours,' David teased. 'Here, have another beer.'

'All of a sudden, I'm peckish. Let's order some fries to go with our beer,' Regu said.

'I thought we won't get a drop of alcohol in Kelantan. Not bad that it is allowed to be sold to non-Muslims,' Samy said.

Suddenly, Kelantan didn't seem all that bad. It was I who was feeling a little sad for myself.

'David, don't come knocking on our door, if Regu gets lucky on his dating App and throws you out,' Samy said.

'I wish,' Regu replied. 'But looks like it's not going to happen. Both the Digi connection and the hotel WiFi suck. They whole of the Internet is against me meeting a nice guy,' Regu replied with a new laugh.

'Hello, you are in Kelantan. Keep your pants on, please!' David reminded Regu.

'Calm down, you guys. It's not all about meeting guys for sex. I've actually made some friends here. And I'm getting better tips on where to eat which is better than TripAdvisor. Gay guys know where to find good food. Have I ever let you down with my restaurant recommendations?'

'Ah! Yes, you just wanted to have small talk with these guys, I see,' Samy said.

'The good news is one of the guys has recommended a great place for breakfast tomorrow. See, it's not all about hooking up with guys for sex.'

We went back to our usual banter. Regu's startling revelation had gone down well with us. We ate the fries and drank our last can of Tiger beer. I wished I could have the same confidence Regu had. But my secret will be mine only.

* * *

The night passed fast. We were fatigued and slept rather soundly. We soon awoke hungry for a big Kelantanese breakfast. One of Regu's chat friends had recommended a *kopitiam* which was *the* must eat place in KB for a local breakfast.

We got into our car, switched on Waze and headed to the kopitiam. Parking was a bit of a problem. Good to see locals' cars, I thought to myself. If the locals were here, it must be a good place, that was my take when going to new restaurants.

It was quite an amazing place. All kinds of local *nasi* dishes and local *kueh* were neatly arranged, as if on a buffet spread. Names of nasi we had only heard of, we now saw laid out on trays, each neatly packed in brown waxed paper and labelled. Among ourselves, we bought enough variety of food to sample the local delicacies. The coffee was ordinary, and I was surprised Samy had not mentioned Starbucks.

We weren't visiting KB to buy its *songket* or *batek* or visit its beaches even. The once popular 'Beach of Passionate Love' had been eroded away and its name had been changed by the Muslim state government to something banal so that the locals would not get any wrong ideas while visiting it.

We left for our overnight stay in Kuala Terengganu early. We wanted to make the most of it for the price we had paid. We were going to take it easy. We had planned to lie under a shade on the beach, read a book and just relax. And that is what we did. We pampered ourselves for a night stay in one of the most exclusive beach front hotel resorts in Terengganu. The resort did not disappoint us for the price we had paid. We only came out of the hotel at night for local food. We didn't want to eat the western food or the upmarket local cuisine in the food outlets in the resort.

Oddly enough, we ended up at an Indian food-stall and had one of the best mutton-curry and rice. Samy had his vegetarian nasi lemak which he seemed to enjoy. The food-stall was run by an elderly Indian woman. Malay-tudung girls in pants served the customers, who were mostly Malays too. What struck me was that there were no halal signs on this food-stall. The east coast food stalls and restaurants were certainly quite different from those in the west coast, where obligatory halal signs hung loudly as if they were part of the décor.

We reluctantly left the best hotel we had ever stayed in. The beach, the bed and breakfast certainly made up for the price we had paid. Like most return trips, our drive back was quieter as heading back to small-town Melaka was rather less enticing. This time round, we saw some of the things we had not seen before along the roadside. But we certainly didn't see the aphrodisiac-peddling makcik on the other side of the road. My request for one last durian stop was not received enthusiastically. A few miles outside Kuantan, David stopped the car near a durian stall and I was the first one out.

Two pakcik were in conversation, sitting behind their durian stand. The durians were rather small and certainly looked like kampung durians. I asked for a durian. One of the pakcik asked me to try a durian, which he had opened. He offered me a few more pods from the same fruit. They were delicious. Just the taste I liked.

I asked him to pick an unopened fruit for me. The pakcik sitting next to him pointed to a fruit. So, I asked the pakcik with the knife to open it. I tasted the first pod from the fruit. It was slightly dry and hard. It was semi-ripe. I complained and said I didn't like it.

The pakcik with the knife replied in Malay, 'Why you listen to him? The fruits are from my trees not his.' I was a little puzzled with the turn of events. The other pakcik remained silent.

David who had been watching the whole scene, added salt to my wound. 'Why didn't you pick up the fruit and shake it? The makcik told you that is how to check if the fruit is ripe. Didn't learn anything ah? Wasted road trip on you lah!'

I asked the durian-tree owner pakcik to choose and open another fruit for me. I didn't want the last fruit for the trip to leave a bad taste in my mouth.

Best Man's Kiss

I thought I heard my doorbell ring. I hoped a kid was not playing. Those of us who cannot afford condominiums had to accept many unsolicited intrusions. Although there had been some surprises. Great when a wrong number turns out to be a great number—but that was rare. The bell rang again. Now really irked by it, I got out of my comfortable chair and went to the door.

I was not expecting anyone and was in no mood for any kind of company. Peering through the peep hole I saw Gina on the other side of the door. *What on earth was she doing here*, I wondered as I opened the door.

'Sorry, Annan. I know I should have called. Hope I'm not disturbing,' she started.

'No, you're not. But what are you doing here. We do have telephones. Is something wrong?'

'That's really you, you know, Annan. That's the only time I ever see you. When someone has died or is in a coma.'

'I gather this is then a special occasion. There's no dead body here and neither one of us is in a coma!' I teased her.

Gina, my little sister, sat on my favourite chair. She did have a way picking the things that were mine. But I have always loved her and was more than willing to let her have them.

'So what brings you to this part of town and to my flat, Gina?' She had not been here for a long long time. And I knew Gina did not really like my neighbourhood, either.

'Next Thursday is my fifth wedding anniversary. We're having a dinner party. So here I am bringing you the invitation in person. You are allowed a date. Bring whoever you want. Be there. We've not seen you for ages.'

* * *

Gina's visit took my thoughts back to Jason. It was only after my third month with Jason that I had told him about my family. It was often such a waste of time telling your boyfriends your background. Most did not make it past the second date. Some guys can be fun but there was so little to say after the sex. And I really wanted to be with someone I could talk to. Although often I had been accused of talking and talking and talking.

The first time I saw Jason was at Jalil's party. In a room filled with men. All professionals. Mid-career executives climbing up the social ladder ever so carefully. You only get to Jalil's parties by invitation. At least two guys must vouch for your credibility. No one under twenty-one was invited. Nothing to do with the age of consent. Just hormones.

Jason was standing at one side of a relatively large hall, surrounded by three young men – all very good-looking. They were in some kind of deep discussion. Odd thing at a party on a Saturday night, all the more so in one of Jalil's parties.

I must have been staring. Jalil touched my elbow and whispered 'The name's Jason'.

I turned to Jalil and saw a mischievious grin on his happy face. 'Want to meet him now or maybe later?' he asked. Knowing my answer will definitely be later.

And I did meet him later and brought him back to my flat. He stayed the night, whatever was left of it, and we got up for brunch.

I watched Jason much of the evening before I was introduced to him. He was in fine form. He had only been in a serious mood with the three guys I had first seen him with. After a few minutes, their talk took on a lighter tone and soon they went their different ways, speaking to other men.

The first thing I asked Jason was what he had been talking about with the other guys. His face changed. I told him that I did not mean to pry and tried to change the subject. But he insisted on telling me what they had been talking about.

'A close friend of ours has died in England. It was AIDS, of course. He was a lovely person. I will miss him. It seems ages ago when I first met him even though its just been twelve years,' he began.

I wished I had not opened my big mouth. *Here I was interested in the bloke and I was sending him into some sad journey down memory lane*, I thought.

'Mike, I guess, will always be one of the loves of my life. We met. Fell in love. Then, we just continued to love each other. We found other men to fall in love with but never stopped loving each other.'

I wanted to steer Jason away from his dead friend and bring him back to the present, and me. 'So where do you work?' I queried casually. This brought him back and we were soon talking about the gyms we went to and what food we avoided. *Good signs*, I told myself.

* * *

Six months passed and Jason and I were still dating each other. We soon got into the routine of catching up with each after our workouts. Neither of us was willing to give up his gym for the other's. I took this as a sign. A sign of what, I was not sure. I felt we still had a distance to go—together. I could not imagine falling in love and, more importantly, staying that way. The magic words still remained unspoken. I was not even sure if he was aware of them.

We were seeing other men. But they were becoming fewer as we spent more time together. The Christmas holidays were drawing close and I would soon be leaving for home in Melaka. My parents had a house in Klebang. It would be no problem inviting Jason home for the Christmas weekend. Many friends had stayed over before. I knew Amma would love to fuss over another man in the house. It would also give Appa and me a welcome break. But more than anything else, deep inside me, I wanted my parents and sister to meet this lovely man I had met and was just about falling in love with.

I tried out the idea with Jason. He thought I was kidding. And was amused with the whole idea—taking a boyfriend home for Christmas and to meet his parents.

'Will I be sneaking into your bed after everyone's gone to bed?' he asked.

'Better still, you get to share my double bed,' I replied.

He had a shocked look on his face. Then he broke into a smile. 'You're kidding, right?' he queried.

'No, there is a double bed in each of the rooms in the house,' I informed him as a matter of fact.

Jason gave some thought to my proposition. 'We have no Christmas celebrations in my house this year. My grandmother died a few months ago. I would hate being home and not having our usual Christmas festivities, especially my mum's Christmas turkey curry.

'You're really inviting me to your home, Balan, aren't you?' Jason suddenly sounded serious.

'Yes, baby, I am!' I replied more tenderly than I had intended.

We looked at each other and moved into each other arms. And before we knew it we were locked in a strong embrace and a deep loving kiss. Probably the most passionate of all the kisses in our young love.

* * *

It was great to go home with Jason. I knew my parents would enjoy having another guest for Christmas. We arrived on Christmas Eve. Just about everything was ready. The big old Christmas tree had been pulled out of the garage and redecorated. My sister, Gina, greeted Jason. After the initial formalities, we went to my room and unpacked. Jason soon complained that he had not bought any presents—feeling guilty seeing the huge Christmas tree in the hall. We set off to the only local decent shopping complex in Melaka town—Mahkota Parade. It was built on reclaimed land. If the Portuguese of olden days returned to Melaka today, they would have wondered why their fort, *A Formosa*. which had once protected their port now stood so far inland!

On our return home, my sister, Gina, who was in her final year at University of Malaya, decided to make Jason her resource person for job opportunities in Kuala Lumpur. He patiently answered her questions, even promising to introduce her to friends who might be able to employ her after her graduation. It pleased my parents that I had brought a friend who could be of help to Gina.

My parents had often asked me to introduce some nice Indian boy to Gina. That, of course, had been a problem for me. Most of the guys I knew would rather be with me than my little sister!

Jason and I had decided we would leave for Kuala Lumpur on Boxing Day. As I was having breakfast alone with my mother, she began to quiz me about Jason. I could sense in which direction the questions were going.

'Amma, I did not bring Jason here to introduce him to anybody. Gina probably has a boyfriend in the university!'

'Balan, he seems like a nice boy. Nothing wrong if he and Gina meet more in KL,' she added.

I told her that it was up to Gina and Jason. I would not have anything to do with it. Jason had given her his mobile phone number. She knew how to reach him.

* * *

After our annual New Year party at good old Jalil's place, I invited Jason to move into my flat. He said he'd think about it. I knew then that he would not. I did not bring up the matter again and he did not give me an answer. I took it as another sign—we both wanted our own space. Just like our own gyms. *Nothing wrong with that*, I told myself.

A few weeks later, Jason told me that Gina had called him. She had invited him out for dinner. I was surprised that she had not invited me along but said nothing. Jason said he would see me after the dinner and give me a detailed account of the evening. I told him I needed no such boring details. We would have better things to do when he got back, I suggested.

I never did find out what they talked about. Jason and I continued our relationship. We were gaining couple status among our friends. It was a warm, comforting feeling. I felt less of the urge to meet new men. I was growing comfortable in my love and Jason did not seem to stray far from me, either.

Late one evening as we lay in bed, Jason said, 'Don't you think it would be a splendid idea if I married Gina?'

I was flabbergasted. I said nothing, not wanting to regret saying something hurtful or that I might later regret. Worse still, I did not want to sound like a possessive lover.

'It makes complete sense,' Jason added. 'We'll keep it in the family. I'll still have you and you'll know that your sister is in good hands. She's a lovely person and she won't mind me spending time with you.'

'Jason, you're gay,' I reminded him.

'I'm sure I can also perform with a woman,' he replied.

'Jason, you cannot be serious!' My voice was hitting the high notes.

'Balan, I was just suggesting. I don't even know if Gina is in love me,' he tried to console me. 'It will get my mother off my back too,' he added.

'Still the very thought, it frightens me,' I told him.

* * *

My mother telephoned me to give the *wonderful news*, as she called it. Jason had proposed to Gina and she had accepted. They were already talking of the wedding day. My mother was checking for an auspicious date. A few minutes later, Jason walked into the flat. From the look on my face he knew that I had already been told. He said he wanted to be the one to tell me. But now he knew that my mother had beaten him to it.

'Balan, this will make it all so much more cosier for us. I do like Gina. And I do like the idea of having children. I love you and we can still spend time together. No one will suspect anything.'

That was the first time he actually said he loved me. Yet, something went cold within me towards Jason. He wanted everything, my sister and me, for himself. I did not know how he could have us both. Jason and I said little about the wedding from then on. My parents thought it was wonderful that my friend was marrying Gina. At Jason's request, I agreed to be his best man.

Jason and I continued to sleep with each other. On the night before the wedding, we made love in a frantic fashion, which neither could explain.

In the morning, we dressed in my bedroom for the wedding ceremony. Jason looked handsome in his bridegroom suit. Here we were, two men who loved each other. In some countries, we could have been on the way to our own wedding. As I adjusted his tie, a strong pang of love surged through my being. I drew him to my body and held him in an embrace I have never held a man before or will ever again. As we kissed, I knew that I would never kiss this man again.

* * *

I did not make it to my sister's and Jason's fifth wedding anniversary. Just like I never went for any of their earlier anniversaries. My mother constantly asks why I see so little of my best friend. My sister assumes something has gone sour between Jason and me. I do not care to know what Jason thinks. He wanted more than he could have. And I was not willing to make a sham of my little sister's life. I had my own to deal with.

Give Us This Day

Larry fell heavily. His left knee twisted badly, and he thought he felt something tear. His rather slim body hurt. He was not expecting this physical assault on his body. They had begun quarrelling and arguing for a few years. The last few months had only gotten worse. Simon had often threatened to hit him when they argued. He had even slapped him on several occasions. This was the first time he had hit Larry with such force.

Matt came by Larry's apartment and took him to the Emergency room in a nearby hospital. Larry sat in a wheelchair waiting for a doctor. He wondered how things had sunk so low with Simon. A home they had shared for almost twenty years had become a boxing-ring. Simon had stormed out of the apartment as Larry lay in pain on the bed he had shared with Simon, the years now feeling like more than a lifetime. Matt said nothing. He had said it all before and he knew Larry would not want to hear what Matt will only be repeating: get rid of Simon.

Finally, a medical officer examined Larry. 'You seem to have torn some ligaments in your knee,' he said.

'What caused you to fall so badly?'

Larry remembered Simon's fist slamming at his cheek and him falling on their bedroom floor. 'I didn't know the floor was wet, I slipped and fell in an awkward way.'

'Did you hit your cheek too, when you fell?'

'I must have,' Larry replied.

The medical officer admitted Larry and informed him that an orthopaedic surgeon would examine him later in the ward.

* * *

Larry arrived at dinner looking exhausted. He had been driving for a couple of hours to get to the restaurant. Larry constantly cursed the traffic jams in Kuala Lumpur. His friends had begun to tease him for a while now that he needed a young man on the side, to look after him and drive him around.

'Simon not with you?' Fred asked.

'Don't ask the obvious, lah,' Matt chipped in.

Matt and those close to Larry knew that things had been going poorly between Larry and Simon. They no longer had to guess whether Simon would join them at their get-togethers. He had stopped coming over the last few months. Larry had confided to them many times. They could not understand why Larry continued to stay and take the abuse. Larry did not need Simon. He was financially stable and well set-up for his old age. Money from some very good investments and pension funds were available to him till his final days. Simon had neither. But he had Larry.

'Larry, you need a new younger lover-boy, lah!' said Matt. Laughter rang all round the table.

'Hey! I'm not kidding. Look at Guna. He's got a young man. So very attentive to Guna's needs. Guna is happy and looking good. They seem to be looking after each other. It's all very symbiotic. It might even be love. Who's to say!'

'Ya, ya! Help find me one lah. I'm still surfing Planet Romeo. Mostly old people here.'

'Aiyoh! You need to download Hornet or Jack'd! All the young lads are there. Just avoid the two M's—masseurs and money boys,' Matt advised.

The food arrived at their table and Larry lost his friends' attention.

* * *

Larry went for social gatherings on his own. Simon began to move away from their mutual friends. He declined to go for social events he had once attended with Larry. Simon had no new friends. His new acquaintances were those who he had met at bars and night clubs. These new acquaintances were never introduced to Larry. Simon slept during the day and disappeared during the nights. Most nights he was too wasted to even go upstairs to their bedroom. In the beginning, Larry lay awake most nights wondering where his partner was and what he was doing. He would hear the key turn in the front door in the early hours of the morning as Simon came home. Soon, it was clear to Larry that something was wrong. Larry was neither naïve nor blind and he soon saw what Simon had succumbed to. Simon was withdrawn and often fidgety. He could not sit still and hold a conversation. He slept through the day and was out throughout the nights.

'This can't go on,' Larry said.

'Nothing is going on. I enjoy going to clubs. I enjoy the music. I love dancing,' Simon said in his defence.

'You know, I'm not referring to that.'

'What else is there to refer to, Larry?'

'The drugs you are taking, Simon. I'm not blind. I can see what it is doing to you. What it is doing to us.'

Simon sat still in silence. The house was quiet except for the murmuring sound of the old air-conditioner. The blue walls with dim lights accentuated a feeling of sadness that now hung heavily within it.

'Let's get help, Simon. Let's rid you of this addiction. We'll go for couple-counselling. Get our relationship back on track.'

'I'm in control, Larry. I know what I'm doing. I know the limits. I can take care of myself.'

'I worry about the company you keep. I don't know any of your new acquaintances. It's them I don't trust. I don't trust what they might do to you. Look at what you've become, Simon!' Larry wanted to stay calm and not break down. He felt he was at his wits' end. He was screaming inside, in pain and in anger.

'You don't have to worry about me or my new friends. Just fuck off, Larry. I can take care of myself,' Simon hissed and walked out of the room.

That ended the argument, for now. It would be repeated in various ways, over the next few months, over the same issue that was beginning to tear the two of them apart.

Larry and Simon had been happy for many years. They were the envy of their gay friends. They were successful in their business and had made a home together. This was what many gay men dreamed of, and others pretended not to envy. Although they were not inseparable, they certainly spent a lot of time together. They did things together. They were very much in love with each other. It was from this love that Larry drew his hope from. That love kept him with Simon and sustained his continued desire to be with Simon, despite being rebuffed. Larry still remembered the young Simon, the twenty-year-old lad, he first loved, and that just made the present Simon almost bearable.

Larry blamed himself for Simon's decline. He had turned a blind eye to Simon's growing nocturnal forays into seedy clubs. Later, Larry began insisting that Simon seek help, but it was too late. Simon paid no heed to Larry's insistence which soon turned to pleas. In his desperation, Larry turned to Simon's family for help.

Sitting in Simon's elder brother's living room, Larry saw the family Catholic altar on one of the walls. A crucifix stood next to a small rectangular framed picture of the Virgin Mary. And in front of them were two burned-out candles. Simon's elder brother called him a *pondan* and a loser. He had disapproved of Simon's sexual orientation and had said that he will come to a bad end. Drug addiction was Simon's wages for his sins, his elder brother declared. His saree-clad unwed sisters sat quietly, too scared of their elder brother to say anything.

* * *

Larry underwent a series of blood tests, X-rays, and an MRI. The surgeon advised him to surgically remove the torn meniscus ligament in his knee. The operation was a simple procedure and necessary. The sooner Larry got it done, the earlier he would be able to walk without any pain.

Three days passed and there was still no sign of Simon at the hospital. Larry had sent him text messages but there were no replies. Simon only turned up on Monday after his weekend binge. Larry was surprised to see him. *So, he did read my messages, he still cared*, Larry thought to himself. Simon looked as if he hadn't slept for days. There were black rings around his dark brown skin. He was all skin and bones. His worn-out T-shirt hung baggy on him. He cut a sorry figure. Simon looked at Larry lying on the hospital bed that he had put him in. Sitting on the side of the bed, he held Larry's hand and softly muttered the words, 'I'm so sorry. I didn't mean to hit you.' This time, Larry lay there in silence. He felt a new numbness to Simon's apology.

Larry looked at Simon sitting in the hospital. He could not remember when they had last held hands or hugged, let alone kiss. All that had come to pass many months ago. Larry could not understand what had happened. Simon seemed lost to him now. The man sitting by him was a stranger.

Larry agreed to the operation. He couldn't imagine being unable to use his two legs. He knew he had to be well. He knew he had to be independent. He knew the Simon he once knew and still loved was no longer the man he could depend on. Simon, these days, was not able to care even for himself.

Simon returned every day for the next three days. He looked remorseful. He cleaned and cared for Larry as he had once done, after Larry's appendicitis operation when they just had become a couple. *He had to put me through this hell, and now takes care of me, to show he still loves me*, Larry thought to himself. They spoke little to each other. They skirted around perfunctory household matters such as the cats that needed feeding. When friends came to visit Larry, Simon would make some excuse and leave. He saw in their eyes the words that had not been spoken against him.

* * *

A Nepali concierge staff brought a wheelchair for Larry to take him for his physiotherapy session. The journey seemed long, going up and down a couple of lifts before arriving at the physio centre. At the physio counter, he was greeted by a young Chinese man. The young man confirmed his patient's name and details and wheeled Larry to an available bed with beige curtains around it.

Larry noticed the therapist's name as he bent to push down the brake on his wheelchair.

'Hi, Alan,' Larry greeted him.

'Hi, Mr Larry. How are you today?' came Alan's reply.

Larry couldn't help noticing Alan's keen eyes and smiling lips. His face was bright and cheerful. *Someone here enjoys his work,* were Larry's first thoughts of Alan. Alan was all business and gentle with the sixty-three-year-old man he was handling. Larry was glad Alan didn't call him uncle. How he hated the word young Malaysians used for any male older than them! He felt worse when older women called him that. Who wants to be related to the whole bloody community!

Alan assisted Larry onto the bed. Alan's strong hands held Larry's legs firmly and helped him lie down. There was a gentleness in the experienced manner that Alan treated Larry's body. It had been a long while since any one had held him in a gentle and loving way. Alan was completely unaware of Larry's thoughts. He was being professional and handling Larry's body with care. The slow leg exercises began. Larry continued to gaze at the young man in front of him, his back towards Larry as he handled Larry's leg. Larry's thoughts were not sexual, they were mostly of gratitude.

Larry hated the thought that he might take more than three months to fully recover. Alan had mentioned that and added that younger people recovered faster. Walking with a brace around his knees and with crutches was not what he had wanted. *Damn Simon*, he thought. *I will have to deal with our shit before we kill each other*, he finally admitted to himself.

The quarrel that fateful day had gone beyond anything Larry had imagined. It was early afternoon. Larry had gone out to discuss a business deal. When he returned, as he was entering his apartment, he heard voices in their bedroom. His first thought was that robbers had entered their apartment. But the door was locked and they were on the eighteenth floor. As he walked towards the bedroom he heard muffled voices and giggles. On hearing Simon's voice, Larry opened the door. Amidst the smell of ganja, he saw three naked men on their bed.

'What the hell is going on Simon?' Larry shouted.

A dazed Simon looked at it.

'How dare you bring ganja and your bloody friends into our house!' Larry continued to shout at Simon. Simon's accomplices without a word began to gather their clothes and slipped out of the bedroom.

'This is my house too, I can bring my friends here, if I want,' Simon finally spoke.

'Not if you are doing drugs with them, Simon. And certainly, not having a drug-induced sex-orgy on our bed. I don't know what you do outside. You certainly cannot bring your drugs and sex-partners into our home,' Larry now spoke calmly and slowly.

'Your boss called, Simon. He said he had enough of your constant absence from work. He asked you not to come back'.

Silence.

'How are you going to pay your bills, Simon?'

Simon began to put on his clothes, giving no reply.

'Where are you going to get money for your addiction?'

On hearing 'addiction', something snapped in Simon. He lunged at Larry and punched him hard on his cheek. Larry, completely unsuspecting of such an assault, fell back, twisted his knee and felt an excruciating pain. Simon stared at his fallen partner and then rushed out of their bedroom.

The heat-lamp was directed at Larry's wounded knee. 'Something troubling you, Mr Larry,' Alan asked. This broke Larry's reverie. Larry broke into a smile. It had been a long while since he had smiled so broadly. He liked the face of the young man talking to him.

'Yes,' was all Larry said. Then changed the subject. 'I'm going to be discharged tomorrow. I'll come back for follow-ups. Can you give me the treatment?'

'Mr Larry, if you come during my shift, I will certainly attend to you,' Alan replied.

'Call me Larry, please.'

Alan nodded.

Larry asked for Alan's mobile number. Larry's gaydar was sending him positive vibes about Alan. He said he would write to Alan to check on his shifts so that he could come at those times. Alan obliged and flashed his very congenial smile. Larry was happy. He hoped that something will come out of these communications.

Larry was back in the ward and thought of Alan. He felt he was being rather forward, asking for Alan's mobile number. Then, Alan's smile confirmed to him that he had not gone a little too far. Alan had handled Larry's body with ease and comfort. Although not in any sexual way, yet Larry felt Alan's gentle hands and it pleased him.

Even though nothing might come out of his desire for Alan, it was a feeling Larry had not felt for a very long time. He liked the feeling of seeing beyond Simon. Simon will have to go. Maybe, a gentle lover, someone like Alan, might come into his life. Larry felt he could at the least dream about it.

Sleeping Demon

The last weekend had not gone well for Manoh, to say the least. Now he sat distracted on his bed. He rarely stayed in his bedroom. The only times when he came up to his bedroom were to have sex, shower or sleep. Here he was, wide awake, alone and with no plans for a shower. What he had thought was behind him had suddenly re-emerged. What he had thought he had managed to push deep into the recesses of his mind suddenly resurfaced and the weekend he had meticulously planned, had collapsed and left him feeling anxious. He had put on a strong face and managed to see the weekend through. He was quite sure even Nathan had not seen the disquiet in him.

* * *

When Nathan heard about Manoh and Santhu he was not surprised. Santhu had all the five requirements Manoh demanded in his men; fair, young, tall, innocent and Indian. Some of Manoh's earlier conquests were not quite men yet and Nathan had often told Manoh that his preference for young boys dangerously bordered on paedophilia and breached the age-of-consent law. To this comment, Manoh would retort, 'There's no age of consent for gay sex in this country.' Nathan would then use his legal background to remind Manoh that the legal age for marriage for men was eighteen. This, of course, was nonsense when it came to gay men, as all homosexual acts were criminalized in Malaysia. Anyway, Santhu, Manoh's business partner's son, who was doing his A-levels, barely looked eighteen.

Nathan himself had been one of Manoh's early conquests. Nathan had just turned twenty when he met Manoh. Within a few months they had become a couple. However, their relationship was doomed from the beginning. Manoh was always on the prowl and did not know the meaning of the word 'monogamous'. And sadly, unlike Dorian Gray, mere mortal Nathan began to age. Nathan was still fair-skinned but no longer young. Now at thirty-five, Nathan could still pass off for a late twenty-something man. But Manoh had gone beyond him. The many years of vegetarianism, teetotaling and evening runs kept his body slim and firm. After more than a decade of their failed relationship, Manoh's and Nathan's love for Kathak music still bound them. Even as they slowly drifted away from each other and were no longer in a sexual relationship, they remained connected despite both of them continuing to have sex with other men. Nathan became Manoh's confidant and listened to his every new encounter.

Manoh was also one of those gay men who could not resist being attracted to straight men. His personal motto was, 'There are no straight men. They had not just met the right gay man.' And Manoh saw himself as the right gay man to the men he was often attracted to. Nathan, however, had to admit that Manoh had a high success rate. Beer and straight porn often made the guys he desired so horny, they could be coaxed to receive a hand job or even receive a blow job. So Manoh got his way with many straight men. And once he had his way with them, they held no interest for him anymore.

'But they do nothing for you!' Nathan had once told him.

And Manoh immediately replied, 'Of course they do, you just don't know how much pleasure I get.'

* * *

Nathan was seated at a banana-leaf restaurant having his afternoon tea when Manoh arrived. Manoh was immaculately dressed in his trademark complete black attire, this time in a T-shirt and denim jeans. Nathan managed to get him out of his tailored slacks when he told him he might be mistaken for an Indian fresh out of an Air Asia flight from India. Manoh's black outfits further accentuated his dark complexion, the exact effect he wanted to project. Unlike many Indian men, Manoh was clean-shaven; no moustache or designer beard, just two prominent side-burns that ran down to his earlobe. The only hair on his face were his rather bushy eyebrows. His hair was cut short and pitch black; dyed every fortnight, a part of his Sunday routine.

After ordering their masala tea and *vadais*, Manoh started talking about Santhu, in his typical fashion.

'Took Santhu for a movie yesterday night. He's so cute.'

'His parents don't mind? A weekday night, even!'

'No, la. They thanked me for taking him off their hands and to a Hindi movie they don't want to watch.'

'Very convenient for you, Manoh.'

Manoh had his mischievous smile on and now it looked like a smirk. Nathan was not very comfortable with what was going on. But he felt he couldn't judge Manoh. 'How are the arrangements for Banu's son's wedding coming along for this weekend?' Nathan asked Manoh, changing the subject.

'Krish has sorted out the arrangements for travel and accommodation. We can go with Saras, Santhu, and him. They have a seven-seater.'

Nathan sensed where this was going. 'I'll stay with my mum in Kuantan. So, no worries about my accommodation,' Nathan told Manoh.

'No worries la, they have a huge bungalow with enough rooms for all of us. Krish is Banu's cousin and she wants us all to stay together in their house. Let's all stay together. Less hassle to go for the dawn wedding ceremony on Saturday.'

* * *

Nathan took a Grab to Manoh's apartment. Krish arrived a few minutes later and they set off once both Nathan and Manoh had put their luggage in the booth. Nathan made himself comfortable at the back row while Manoh promptly placed himself next to Santhu, in front of him. The three-hour car drive was uneventful. Besides the driver, everyone was busy with their mobile phones. Somewhere along the journey, Santhu had lain on Manoh's ever-ready shoulder and fallen asleep, an earphone still in his ear and the other half in Manoh's. Manoh must have been as happy as a dog with a new bone. The traffic was kind until they arrived right smack into after-office-hour Friday traffic. They arrived at Banu's bungalow at Teluk Cempadak while evening tea was still being served.

There certainly were many people at the house. Most of them seemed like relatives and Manoh and Nathan were probably the only guests. The bride's mother, Banu, was a secondary-school classmate and they had remained close friends. They were the only three Indian students in the Form Six Arts class. So what started as a form of security for the three Indians gradually grew into a long friendship. They got to know Banu's husband, Seelan, over the years. First, he seemed a little distant from his wife's male bachelor friends. But he soon warmed up over beer, commando chips and gin rummy.

They loved Banu's fiery commando chips, something she had picked up from a chef from her father's social and recreational club. The three of them used to go there for a weekly lunch at the club. Banu could sign for the food through her father's membership. Manoh and Nathan had their own private joke about the underwear-less hot spicy chips stir-fried with anchovies. This weekend there will be no gin rummy. There certainly will be a free flow of beer, but commando chips won't be served either.

Banu had already organized the sleeping arrangements for them. Krish and wife would be in a room and the remaining three guests in their own rooms. Nathan was glad to be on his own. They were all left to their own devices till dinner and then to a good night's rest before the very early morning wedding ceremony at the biggest Hindu temple in Kuantan, the next day.

Dinner was a lavish event. Banu had ordered food from the most popular and expensive Indian food caterers in town. An aromatic array of southern and northern Indian cuisine assaulted their senses. A whole roasted lamb was the main attraction for every discerning Indian palate. This would be quite a contrast to the vegetarian food that would be served at the temple the following morning. At some point during the meal, just about everyone would have made their way to the roasted lamb, even the cholesterol-laden guests.

Santhu was inseparable from Manoh since the time they had arrived. They sat next to each other, still sharing a head-phone set. Nathan knew exactly what Manoh was doing. The young lad was unaware, enjoying the attention from the older man. There were a few young people at the dinner, but Santhu showed no interest in mingling with them. Anyway, they, too, seemed to have found cliques of their own.

After the meal, each of them made their way to their rooms. Manoh yearned to spend the night with Santhu. He decided he would lay the foundations for future explorations during this weekend. He went to Santhu's room and knocked on the door. A shirtless Santhu greeted him.

'Hi, Uncle Manoh. Anything?'

'I was wondering if you want to listen to some music in my room? It's a big bed and it's comfortable enough for two.'

Quite excited at the prospect of spending more time with Manoh, Santhu closed the door behind him and followed Manoh. A few minutes later, Saras wanting to check how her son had settled in for the night, came by and found his room empty. She guessed that he might be with Manoh. On her second knock, Manoh opened the door and she saw Santhu sitting on the bed.

'I thought I'd find you here. Don't stay up too late. We have an early morning tomorrow. Manoh, don't spoil him. He needs his sleep,' she said and left.

'Good night, Amma,' Santhu called after her.

Manoh closed the door and went back to the bed and put on the other earphone. After a few songs Manoh asked Santhu if he wanted to sleep in Manoh's room. 'We can continue listening to songs and fall asleep.' Santhu agreed. Manoh suggested that they strip down to their underwear and get comfortable. Manoh was surprised to see that Santhu wore white briefs. *His mother is still buying his underwear*, Manoh thought. For Manoh, white underwear was impractical and it had gone out of fashion a couple of decades ago. He kept his thoughts to himself.

'These are good songs, Uncle Manoh.'

'No need to call me Uncle when you are alone with me. Call me Manoh. I don't mind.'

Santhu didn't say anything. He had always called Manoh 'uncle' as that was how his Amma had told Santhu to address Manoh.

After a while, Santhu slipped under the light blanket and began to doze off. Manoh looked at Santhu for a long time. He took the earphones off Santhu's ear and the young man turned on his side, facing away from Manoh. Manoh slowly manoeuvred Santhu to lie on his back again. Manoh moved his head towards Santhu's groin. Manoh saw the slight bulge in Santhu's underwear. He closed his eyes and moved his face toward his target to inhale the odour of the boy. Suddenly, he stopped. His mind flashed back a scene that had once plagued him, many times before, even after the source of his misery had gone away from their home. What had started as play and a secret only the two shared turned to revulsion. It was all very exciting in the beginning. He knew he was doing something forbidden but Devi *Akka* had started it and he did not want to refuse her. Soon it became frequent, and he felt used but could not stop her. She frightened him by threatening him. She said she would tell his mother that he had been a naughty boy and had done things to her. For a few years this scene returned to torment him. It only faded away a few years ago. He had since forgotten all about it. Now, as the scene played out in his mind, he saw himself again under the family dining table.

A long table cloth is hanging very low, almost covering the table legs. He is under the table. He sees her legs. She's standing ironing clothes. Her legs are parted. He senses her impatience. He moves forward. He knows what is expected of him. As if in a trance he raises the table cloth and her short skirt. There is no obstacle. He moves his head forward and he can smell her womanliness. He begins and hears her moan. He knows when he can stop.

Manoh pulled his head back in a start. He lay awake on his pillow, afraid to close his eyes.

* * *

It was still dark outside when everyone came downstairs. The dawn wedding ceremony was set at an auspicious time and they had to get to the temple soon. Manoh was dressed in a new black kurta top with a black bottom for the wedding. 'Another kurta set bought from Fabindia?' Nathan asked. Manoh gave no reply.

Nathan looked fondly at Manoh. He couldn't help thinking how handsome Manoh looked. He looked as attractive as when Nathan had first met him. Nathan quickly killed the thought. 'That way madness lies,' Nathan muttered a line from his Form Six Shakespeare class to himself and walked behind Manoh.

'Hope the night went well.'

Again, another silence.

Manoh did not return the expected smile. Nathan wondered what had happened. He dropped the subject. They got into the waiting car and left for the temple. Everyone was back in the same seats as the day before.

The wedding ceremony proceeded like clock-work. Everyone there was in their best attire and the women were decked in gold. All this jewellery would be returned to the safe boxes in the banks the next day. Now, all eyes were on the bride and groom on the dais. The wedding ceremony climaxed with the groom tying the *thali* around the bride's neck that was already bedecked with an elaborate gold necklace and gold chains. The incessant sounds from the *nathaswaram* and the beating of *tavil* drums rang out.

Manoh remained his unusually quiet, new self, only making brief small talk with acquaintances seated near him. He only spoke briefly, when spoken to. He had not bitched about a single person or commented on any of the young men looking fabulous in their traditional Indian outfits. Nathan was bored. He shifted his attention to the eye-candy among the guests. He didn't know anyone here. The attractive younger men Manoh normally relished, seemed to have lost their appeal this morning and Santhu didn't seem to be the cause, either. Santhu was seated next to Manoh paying no attention to the ceremony or Manoh but lost in his mobile phone.

Now a grand Indian vegetarian breakfast of *thosai, idly, poori, vadai* and Indian sweetmeats lay before the guests. With so much to go round, meat was not missed and Nathan, certainly did not miss it, having not tasted it since birth. This was a family tradition he had never complained about. The guests also knew that the wedding dinner which will follow in a few hours will out-do what they had the night before.

The day of the wedding had gone by fast. During the dinner, both Nathan and Manoh were kept busy by some familiar faces. No one asked them when it would be their turn to marry. They had both gone past what was considered the marriageable age and being husband material. The aunties and uncles had moved on to hounding other younger grooms-to-be.

Nathan watched Manoh talking to one of the young men among the dinner guests. They had met him at another wedding a few months ago. Nathan knew that Manoh had met him before for sex. Sitting among other guests, Nathan noticed Manoh leave the room and the young man following him.

Once in the room, the young man unzipped Manoh's pants and pulled out his cock. Manoh closed his eyes and was lost in the pleasure he was receiving. Once done, he pulled up his pants which lay around his ankles and gently kissed the young man on his lips. 'Glad to see you again, let's go back to the crowd before we are missed,' he said sweetly. While walking back to the main dinner area, Manoh sighed relief. He felt he still had it in him. He hadn't lost his touch. He wondered what had happened to him the night before.

Nathan knew that Manoh would give him a detailed account if anything had transpired the night before when time permitted. All the socializing and eating sent them to their beds by midnight, even as the last guests drove out the house gates. Manoh was exhausted by early evening, not having slept properly the night before, and soon he was sound asleep.

By mid-morning they were bidding a very tired Banu and Seelan their goodbyes. The bride and groom were still in the bridal suite that had been set up in one of the many rooms in the house. 'The highway traffic is heavy and unpredictable during the weekends. It is best we arrive in KL by early afternoon,' Krish announced, apologizing for their early departure. The drive back was very much like the drive from Kuala Lumpur. After about three hours, Krish dropped them off at Manoh's apartment. Everyone shook hands except Manoh who gave Santhu a warm hug and said his goodbye. As the car drove off, Nathan could not wait any longer.

As soon as they entered Manoh's house, 'Tell me, la, what happened? Two nights and nothing to report?' Nathan burst out.

* * *

Nathan was not surprised with the details that Manoh gave about his brief encounter with the young man during the wedding dinner. But he found it unbelievable that nothing had happened between Manoh and Santhu the night before. It was totally out of character for Manoh, Nathan thought. *How strange! How un-Manoh-like*! Nathan knew that if anything had transpired, even if Santhu had given him a chaste peck on his cheek, Manoh would not have held back. He never lost an opportunity to boast of a sexual conquest.

Manoh had not fully recovered from what had happened on the first night in Kuantan. He thought it was all in the past. Something within him had triggered it to re-surface. It had lain silent for so long that he had thought it was gone. Why it had returned to haunt him now, he didn't know. The sleeping demon seemed to have awakened. His quick sexual escapade during the wedding dinner was like old times. But every time his thoughts strayed to Santhu, he felt his old fear and his mind played out the scene he was trapped in.

Manoh could not understand what was happening to him. He was not doing something he had not done before. There had been many men from whom he had got what he had wanted, and in many different ways. From the seemingly innocent get-the-men-drunk approach so they are completely relaxed and he could have his way with them to the more exploitative methods. Once Manoh had given an uncooperative young man a cup of coffee with a small dose of Valium mixed in it. The unsuspecting young man soon fell asleep and Manoh had been delighted. He had gone on to take photos of the young man in slumber, fully unclothed waist downwards. Nathan was one of the beneficiaries of these semi-naked photos. Manoh had not stopped to consider the implications of his actions. When Nathan had tried to tell him, Manoh just laughed it off, 'It's just for my collection.' What he had planned to do with Santhu that night was nothing near to what he had done before. He merely wanted to gently touch Santhu and lay his face on Santhu's cock and inhale deeply while giving release to his already hard cock.

Manoh broke his silence and told Nathan. 'You're gonna be surprised, man. Nothing happened. I had got both of us down to our underwear and somehow I just could not go any further. I just watched Santhu sleep and then finally dozed off. Such an anti-climax after all that planning. I think I need to see a doctor,' Manoh said, a little distracted. Exactly for what purpose, Manoh did not say.

Ghosts

Ganesh got off the bed, his eyes still filled with sleep. It had been a busy Saturday at the bank. He had not planned to sleep till so late in the evening. It was supposed to have been a nap. It was nearly nine o'clock and Navin would soon arrive. They would be going out for a drink and some of the light-hearted conversation they had enjoyed since their secondary schooldays.

He looked at the urn on the table. His father's ashes had been on that table for the last three years. His friends didn't think it quite normal for a son to keep his father's ashes in such close proximity. But that had been one of his father's last requests. He had wanted to be in Malaysia on his birthday in 2020, one way or the other.

'Good evening, Appa,' Ganesh greeted his father's ashes aloud. *Tomorrow you won't be here and I shall be truly alone,* he thought. Ganesh had grown used to the simple urn that held his father's remains. He was the only child of a passionless marriage. The urn never failed to bring his father's image to mind and this always led to thoughts of his mother.

Ganesh had tried to cope with his father. It was his mother that he loved. For her, he would give anything and everything. Yet she made no demands of him. She was there. She had been there for his father and was there for him, as well. *Amma and Appa*, he thought to himself and sighed. He loved them and missed them still. His father had once told him that he was their love child. He wished his parents had saved some of that love to sustain their own relationship.

'Don't get married,' his father had advised. 'Ganesh, you'll achieve more on your own. Children don't continue in their parents' ways. They start what they wish. You must make a name for yourself. Let other people make babies. Make your mark in whatever you do. We need Indians among the higher-ups in this country. You will be remembered for your achievements, not for your children.'

'Appa, tomorrow, you set yourself free, or whatever is left of you,' he said aloud, and the sound of his voice startled him. Ganesh wondered if death did actually set one free. His mind was still feeling too fuzzy to get philosophical and he brushed the thought aside.

He remembered that Navin would be arriving soon and went to have his shower. He decided that they'd drive to the beach at Morib early the next morning to carry out his father's wishes. Navin would be spending the night at the apartment.

Ganesh had made no arrangements for any kind of puja for his father before throwing his ashes into the sea. His father had not wanted him to perform any religious ceremonies. It was to be a simple act of renting a boat, sailing a few miles from the shore, and pouring the ashes into the surface of the sea.

Navin arrived just as Ganesh finished dressing. *Well timed*, he thought. A good omen, too. He showed Navin the guest room and once his guest had freshened up after his long drive, they left for their favourite pub, Rogues, in Petaling Jaya. Ganesh volunteered to drive.

'I had *thosai* and teh-tarik on the way here,' Navin told his friend and host. 'I wanted to tapau two thosai for you, but I only remembered just as I was leaving. The eating-shop was crowded . . .'

'Excuses, excuses,' Ganesh cut in. 'Thanks anyway, Nav. It was a hectic day at work. No time for lunch. I had two packets of Instant Classic Maggi Mee when I got home. We can get some supper later. I know a hawker stall that is open till late at night. It's in one of those complexes. Rats still scuttle between the cooks' feet and their kitchens are as filthy as ever. But the food has not lost its distinctive flavour.'

Ganesh passed his ID card through the electronic detector. A blue light blinked. He opened the door and entered. Navin followed Ganesh after passing the detector. The detector was the bane of many Malay men as it denied them entry into pubs, if they were Muslim. Most pub-owners, grateful that they could continue their business in a nation moving towards fundamentalism, found it to be only a minor irritation. Any Muslim entering their premises through his own devices was not their responsibility.

The pub was three-quarters full when they arrived. They found themselves a table away from any speakers on the wall. The music was a bit too loud, but fortunately, the DJ had the same taste in music as they did. This was one of the main reasons they often came back here. Once, Navin had requested Bryan Adams's early-nineties hit 'Everything I Do, I Do It for You', and the disc-jockey announced that he'd have to look for it from his CD archives.

A waiter came to their table, and they ordered two pints of Carlsberg. When their beer arrived, they drank a toast to each other's health and a pleasant evening.

'I've decided to buy a house in Seremban,' Navin started. 'I'm thinking of getting the loan from your bank,' he said.

'Hey, no problem. I know the manager of the housing loans department. I'm sure it should be all right. It would be nice if it were my bank!' Ganesh laughed.

The Saturday night crowd was slowly coming in. Navin was spotted by one of the guys. Navin waved weakly at the new arrival. The man came over to their table. Navin introduced Ganesh and Rashid.

'Looks like you've got yourself a new friend,' Rashid said.

'No, no, not a new friend. Ganesh and I knew each other in secondary school,' Navin corrected Rashid, rather uncomfortably.

'Nice meeting you, Nav. Got to go. I'm with friends tonight.' He turned to Ganesh and said it was nice meeting him. Then returning his eyes to Navin, he said, 'It's good to see you again. It's been two years. I've missed you. Call me, won't you?' Then Rashid moved away. Navin shifted uncomfortably in his chair.

Ganesh ordered another pint. Navin said that he had had enough to drink and volunteered to drive.

Ganesh looked at Navin and sensed his discomfort. 'Nav, are you all right?' Ganesh asked.

Navin nodded but said nothing.

'It's been a long day for both of us, so why don't we go back to the apartment,' Ganesh suggested.

'Let's stay awhile. I do have something to tell you.'

'No probs.'

Navin sighed and began, 'It's just that you are my best friend and I want to share something really important to me.'

Ganesh began to feel uneasy. Navin seemed far away and he wanted the Navin he knew.

'I'm buying the house with Siva. We've decided to live together. I want you to know that we're lovers. We have been for nearly two years.'

Ganesh just managed to say, 'Oh dear!' It was a surprise. Navin had mentioned Siva before. Yet, they had never met. This was Navin speaking to him. They had been friends since Form Six. All this while, he had never known.

Ganesh wanted to say something. He didn't want to sound naive. But it was a surprise. He didn't want to sound as if he were still a school kid in the early years of the century. It was 2020, he thought to himself. 'Look, Nav, I'm not judging you. I know it's your life.'

'It is. And it hasn't been easy. Telling you this is not easy, either.'

'Nav, I *am* your friend. I care about you. Shit! I love you dearly.'

Navin managed a smile. 'Thanks, Ganesh. I'm relieved.'

'Why?' Ganesh asked, after a short pause.

'Why what?'

'Why are you gay? What about the girls you went out with? It must have been that awful Eurasian girl who put you off women!' Ganesh said, with a slightly mocking grin.

'Don't be silly,' Navin giggled. 'I think I'll have another beer after all,' he added.

'I'll tell you how I decided to give up women,' Navin started. 'Sleeping around was quite exciting at the beginning. I was quite happy sleeping with either a man or a woman. I had no complaints about the sex. But I grew to like it less with women. It was usually after I had come that my problem began. I often had nothing to say to the woman I'd just had sex with. I enjoyed less and less being with them. Often a guy would make some excuse and leave just after sex. But the women wanted to nuzzle up to me and fall asleep. It was easier if I was at their place, I could simply get dressed and go home. But they often ended up at my apartment.

There were many times when I woke up in the morning and I wasn't sure if the person lying next to me was a man or a woman. One morning, after a night of exhausting sex, still drowsy with sleep, I let my hands stray between my partner's legs expecting to feel a hard cock. But all I got was sticky fingers. What I really wanted to find was a cock. I got out of bed and headed for the shower. I was hard but had no interest in the woman in my bed.

The turning point finally arrived when I just could not come with a woman. I actually had to fake my orgasm. That ended sex with women for me.

'I spent the next few weeks very much by myself. I also decided that I'd had enough of casual sex with strangers. I wanted a lover. A man. I'm afraid Rashid was part of that search. I did not mean to hurt him. My search came to an end many months later when I met Siva. I had gone to a pub on gays' night and there he was. I had seen him on campus years ago, but I never thought he was gay.

Well, Ganesh, the rest, as many would say, is history. Sounds like such a cliche. But I've stopped sleeping around since. And I like it. Siva makes it easy for me. He's a good man.' Navin was beaming now.

It was nearing midnight. Ganesh and Navin were feeling light-headed. Ganesh suggested they skip supper and Navin agreed. The drive back was quick. Once in the apartment, they agreed to share one last can of beer for the night.

'Does anyone else know?' Ganesh asked.

'Just some of our gay friends,' Navin replied.

'How are you going to explain buying a house with Siva to your mother?'

'I'm not telling her.'

Ganesh looked at Navin. He wasn't sure what to say. He decided to remain silent this time. Neither his family nor his nation would accept his love for Siva. Navin's news hung heavy on Ganesh. The news had not hit him dramatically like a punch in the gut or a knee in the groin. It was like a dull pain, and he couldn't quite place the source. It disturbed but did not hurt. It had been a long night. He felt confused. He felt exhausted now.

Navin just sat, taking small gulps of beer. He had shared his secret with his friend. So, Ganesh finally knew. Navin could relax. He felt maybe now he could talk about Siva to Ganesh. Maybe not quite yet. He would wait and watch Ganesh. If Ganesh asked, he would tell.

'I don't know about you, but I'm off to bed,' Ganesh said. 'We need to get up early tomorrow.' Ganesh looked at his watch and corrected himself, 'More like today,' he added. He bid Navin good night and went to his bedroom.

Ganesh was tired but could not sleep. He remembered the way Rashid looked at Navin. Navin was important to Ganesh. He wanted to understand. If he couldn't, then he'd just accept. He was glad he wasn't in love. *Appa was right, being in love seems like such a strain on one's energy*, he thought. Giving himself completely to his work had its rewards. He was just two rungs away from the branch manager's position. But it wasn't just a dog-eat-dog world, as certain dogs still got their bones placed in their mouths. Yet he knew he was heading upwards. He worked hard and kissed the right asses, if he needed to.

Ganesh lay in bed waiting for sleep. He began to grow restless. Even as he tried to get some sleep, he felt tense. He turned on his stomach and began to rub himself against the mattress. As he grew hard, he relaxed and soon fell asleep.

The sound of his alarm awoke him. It was seven. Ganesh went to Navin's bedroom. He knocked gently. 'I'm awake, Ganesh, come in,' Navin's voice called.

'Didn't you sleep well?' Ganesh asked.

'I did. I slept quite soundly, thanks,' Navin replied with a broad smile. 'In fact, I've already made some coffee. I was just sitting here on the bed trying not make any noise that might wake you.'

'Silly you. Let's have some coffee then.'

After a cup of coffee, Ganesh showered and got ready to leave. He stood in front of the urn. The small urn held all that had been his father. He'd hold his father in the palms of his hands and finally send him off over the waters, and back to wherever he had come from.

The drive to Morib took less than an hour. Navin drove. Ganesh held the urn. Ganesh remembered his father's description of holding Ganesh just after his birth. His father had often told him that he had held Ganesh in the palms of his hands. Now Ganesh held his father in his.

Navin negotiated the hire of a motorboat with a driver. Ganesh instructed the driver to go a couple of miles out into the Straits of Melaka. They travelled for about twenty minutes. When they seemed far enough from the shore, Ganesh asked the driver to switch off the engine. He looked at Navin. They had not spoken since they got into the boat.

'I think we're far enough out,' Ganesh said.

'Do you have to say a prayer or something before you set the ashes onto the water?' Navin asked.

'No, Appa said I should just open the urn and pour the ashes on the waves. I've grown used to having him with me. I shall miss him. I didn't think I would.'

A tight knot moved up Ganesh's throat, strangling his words. He looked at the urn, then looked at Navin. Ganesh had chosen Navin, his oldest friend, to be with him on this occasion, when he spent the last minutes with his father. Navin moved towards Ganesh and stood beside him in silence.

Ganesh opened the urn. Slowly and very gently, he tipped the urn and his father's ashes flowed gently onto the water and began to spread. The waves carried them away. Soon they were all gone. Ganesh closed the urn and dropped it into the sea. 'Goodbye, Appa. Do rest now,' Ganesh bade him.

Navin moved towards Ganesh and they held each other. Ganesh kissed Navin on his cheek and broke the embrace.

'Thanks for being here, Nav. You know . . .'

'Don't, Ganesh, I'm more than glad to be here with you.'

Once ashore they decided to walk along the beach. They took off their shoes and walked on the warm sand. No one would have guessed what they had just done.

'Today, Sunday twenty-sixth August 2020, Appa would have been sixty-nine. I have grown to love him. He's been dead three years but has become closer and closer to me. He was not easy to live with. He was even less easy to love. He was different and often I could not understand him. Often, I stopped trying to.

Nav, it's my turn to tell you a secret. Looks like we are setting our ghosts free with Appa's ashes.'

They continued walking along the beach. Navin wasn't sure what Ganesh was going to say next. They had known each other for more than fifteen years and neither had guessed at any hidden part of each other's lives.

'Appa was rather eccentric and zealously committed to certain beliefs. He made no compromises about them. His biggest problem was that, as he grew older, he changed his ideas about some things he had once dearly believed in. For his change of mind, my mother and I had to pay the price, too.

Appa was born in 1951. He was very much of the flower power generation. Born into a relatively well-to-do family, he had an overseas university education and in the seventies was almost completely an Anglophile. A change came upon him, rather gradually. He started reading a lot of classical Indian texts. He began to talk about being Indian.

He didn't quite like the idea of losing his identity. He said that he accepted most of the principles of Mahathir's wonderful vision back in the nineties. But he wanted to be a Malaysian Indian. Not just a Malaysian. He then decided to put his beliefs into practice. I was the first person to feel Appa's new fervour to be Indian, when I was still a kid.

One day he called me and informed me that he'd decided to change my name. Boy, was I shocked! I had been Michael for the fourteen years of my life and my father had suddenly decided to change my name. I think I was too shocked to say anything. He said he was giving me an Indian name. The Christian name would have to go. This just added another item to my parents list of arguments.

Two weeks later, I found myself in front of a magistrate and my name was officially changed from Michael to Ganesh. Ganesh paused and looked at the surprised look on his friend's face. Trying to break the sudden odd silence, he added: 'Guess my father thought the name would also give me a helping hand for the future. Appa attempted to obliterate our past completely. He didn't even want to be reminded that he was once a flower child. I tried to remind him of the Indian influence on the Beatles and the West. But he was no longer interested.

'I'm afraid Amma was lost somewhere in my father's past. I am quite sure he still loved her. She just could not keep up with him. Maybe she no longer wanted to. As Appa and Amma drifted away from each other, I tried to love her more. She was always warm and generous to me. She was always giving. Even her withdrawal was a form of giving.

'When Amma lost her battle with Appa over my name, she slowly began to withdraw into herself. Their violent outbursts grew less frequent as Amma refused to be drawn into Appa's schemes and decisions. She cooked, took care of us, and read her books. She declined her friend's invitations and asked no one to our home. Her only trips out of the house were her weekly Saturday trips to the market, supermarket, and a second-hand bookshop from where she bought her books. She continued her weekly outings until she suddenly took ill and withdrew completely from our lives. I knew then that another woman could never take her place in my life.

'Michael or Ganesh, I still felt the same. My father thought it would be a good idea for me to transfer to a new school to start my new life as Ganesh. So off I went to a new school, and I became Ganesh to everyone.

'He eloquently justified his choice of the new name for me. Ganesh. After the Hindu god, Lord Ganesha. He said it was a good name. It was the embodiment of success, good living, prosperity and peace. He said that the name would help me build my personality. He hoped that I, like Lord Ganesha, would overcome all difficulties.

'Nav, you must admit it is a good name. I do hope some good fortune continues to rub off on me. I'm not complaining about my life. It's not too bad. I'm going to look out for the prosperity my father had in mind for me.'

Navin surprised himself by saying, 'Your father worried quite unnecessarily. There has been no mixing of races. There's been no blending of races. There's no melting pot here in Malaysia. Nobody's been willing to give up any part of themselves.'

Before Ganesh could say anything Navin continued, 'Did your father stop believing in Christianity, too? He wasn't merely switching ordinary names, you know? From an archangel's name you were given a Hindu god's name,' Navin added.

'Appa was never a believer. He grew up in a Christian family and after his marriage, he just drifted away from it. He was too far removed from his two sisters and, anyway, he couldn't care less what they thought, let alone listen to my mother's protests. The name meant nothing to me. I had not been to church from the time I was three years old.'

Navin and Ganesh continued walking along the beach. There were a few people selling things at the Sunday morning market. A small crowd gathered around the vendors. As they drew closer, they could see an old Indian man displaying his wares. As they drew closer, they saw that they were idols of Hindu gods and goddesses. They were mostly icons of Lord Ganesha, the elephant-head god, in a variety of sizes.

Navin and Ganesh looked at each other in amazement. They moved towards the stall. The old man looked at them.

'Do you want to buy an idol of Lord Ganesha?' he asked in Tamil. 'He'll bring you prosperity,' the soft-spoken old man added.

Navin told the old man his friend's name. The old man broke into a broad smile. He picked one of the idols and gave it to Ganesh. It was not very big. As Ganesh held it in his palms, it felt warm.

Navin asked the old man what the price was. 'No charge,' replied the old man. 'Take care of your father,' he told Ganesh.

Sex and Politics in the Time
of Lockdown

When the Covid-19 pandemic struck, it brought the world to the kind of standstill like no one had ever experienced. Nations enforced new laws and procedures to keep people homebound. Things that were once taken for granted suddenly felt like a privilege. Two friends, Deva and Surin, felt isolated and alone. Over many years of friendship, they had met up a few evenings a week for drinks and dinner. Their friendship was seeded in an unlikely place, a gay dating website. They met for coffee and surprised themselves by not taking the next step of going to bed. A congenial friendship blossomed, and the idea of sexual intimacy dissolved.

The Emergency Movement Control Order (EMCO) kept them in their respective homes, otherwise they would have been at their favourite Mamak restaurant having a teh-tarik and whatever took their fancy that evening. Instead, each was in his home. Receiving text messages on their mobile phones, watching shows on satellite television, or watching YouTube videos.

Deva could not take the silence and watch the idiot box any longer and decided to call Surin. Surin's home phone rarely rang. Surin knew it would be family, Deva, or a scam caller. Deva, he knew, preferred the old-fashioned landline phone to the smaller mobile phones.

They exchanged their routine preliminaries, and Deva went straight into his philosophical mode.

'It's World War Three, I tell you. We are under curfew and each day a new regulation is imposed on us. Who would have thought this global war would be fought between man and a virus?' Deva said.

'Trust you to see it that way,' Surin replied. He was sitting in the living room of his two-bedroom apartment, which he shared with his older single sister. She was unaccustomed to having her brother in the apartment for the whole day, and preferred to stay in her bedroom and watch her Tamil movies on Astro on her own television set.

'There is talk that we are paying a price for some leak in highly secret laboratories. Look at us, chatting on the phone or texting each other throughout the day.'

Deva poured himself another shot of whiskey and added some ice cubes. Deva had his house to himself and could do as he pleased. There were empty potato chips and groundnut packets on the side table next to him.

'Just what price are we paying?' Surin wondered but did not want to go any further in that direction. 'I admit, chatting in person is better, any time. My fingers are beginning to hurt from all this texting.'

'Today, we would have been at Mydin Restaurant having our teh-tarik and nasi lemak or my favourite *nasi goreng telur mata kerbau . . . Saptahchiah*? What did you have for dinner?'

'A Grab guy brought my nasi goreng telur mata kerbau. Still not eaten it.' He laughed. 'All the food outlets are closed by 8 p.m. My dinner was delivered at 7.30.'

'Cute guy? Did you tip him?' Deva could not help teasing his friend.

'Cashless and contactless. Another new thing. At least for me! He hung our dinner orders on the gate. Couldn't see his face through the helmet and mask.'

'Looks like this one got away.'

'This EMCO is driving me up the wall. I'm wearing out the floors in my apartment.'

'Missing your fun dates? No sex, is it?' Deva teased Surin.

'Sex? What's that? I've gone into repeat mode on all the porn sites and have to resort to Twitter.'

'Remember Manjam? Light years ago.'

'Yes. MIRC, then Planet Romeo, and then Grindr. My sex lifelines. Yes. The wonderful world of Internet hook-ups.'

'Guess we won't *konek* face to face for a while. I'm keeping so many guys in my KIV list. After EMCO la.'

'I found a guy I could not resist. Hotels all closed. I had car sex last Saturday night. With a young Malay guy—'

'Malay guy? You kept that juicy story to yourself for two days? So, unlike you!'

'Was a little embarrassed to tell even you, la. I know you will scold me for being a little reckless—'

'Reckless? Nothing can hold you down! You do realize that we are in lockdown?'

'He showed his Covid-19 vaccination status.' Surin laughed. 'Got both his doses too. Dev, his spoken *inglis* was sooooo good. I couldn't resist—'

Deva laughed. 'You resist? What did Oscar say about temptation? That is so you! Anyway, that's not the kind of oral sex you want—'

'I want! I want! I want! Oh! Did I want it, and got it too! Surin laughed then added, 'he drove a Proton Exora, very convenient.'

'Very patriotic of him. Malaysia *Boleh*! *Surin pun boleh.*'

'Lots of room in the back, not like my Myvi.'

'Enough about the car. Where did you guys meet?'

'We parked our cars in a dark secluded shophouses area. Then I got into his car.'

'How many EMCO regulations did you break?'

'Don't remind me. I was really scared the police might catch us—'

'Clearly not enough to keep you at home.'

Surin laughed. 'Yeah.'

'So, no mask even?'

'While sex? No lah. Crazy ah? Like giving blowjobs with condom on.'

Deva laughed. 'JAKIM catch you then you know.' The government's Islamic moral policing of Muslims was a bane of all fornicators.

Surin went back to talking about his sex-date. The two men had not met up with men, let alone any new man for sex for a while. Surin could not help but boast to Deva. Deva listened in envy.

'A local uni student. Quite a fun guy. Experienced even.'

'Ah, ok. Less work for you.'

'Now doing his internship. Impeccable English, Dev. I think from *atas* family too.'

Deva moved their conversation to their usual routine of gauging if the first date had potential for more meet-ups, or even a fling.

'Boyfriend material or fuck buddy material?'

'ONS material,' Surin sighed.

'Small cock?' Deva let out a wicked laugh.

'Not that, lah! Quite decent size. Clean.'

'*Sunat mah.*'

'He's going back to Kuantan once this MCO is over. Looks like I have to go on the prowl again. But am staying away from Indians for now.'

'Oi! You, racist. We are Indians, lah.'

While listening to Deva, Surin took a couple sips of cold beer. He rarely liked making long telephone calls. But he found that he was enjoying himself. He was slow to respond to Deva.

'Ei! You still there?'

'Ya, Ya. Taking a sip of my Carlsberg.'

Deva had grown tired of listening to Surin's latest conquest, and changed the subject to his favourite topic, after sex—politics.

'Can't believe we're in a pandemic. We started so well. Then the bloody change of government. Our PM and his self-serving shitty cronies. Now the shit has really hit the fan.'

'It is like a war, like you said.'

'It is. We are fighting for our lives. The politicians are trying to save their own skins. A new government during this time of crisis. Those buggers are greedy for power and the people are raising white flags and black flags in despair.'

'Now we have this new flag-raising thing and people setting up food banks. I'm not too sure about these free food banks.'

'Why not? People are suffering. Many people need help. We have to help each other.'

'I see lots of freeloaders out there. The poor have too much dignity to come and take these handouts. Have you seen some of the videos? One carload comes and *sapu* all the food! Bloody greedy lot.'

'There are bad apples everywhere. Greed is almost our national trademark. People are losing their jobs. My friend's wife has lost her job, and now she's baking sourdough bread for sale.'

'Oh dear. Baking seems to have also hit a new high as a hobby. Some guys are even baking banana bread and cakes. Good grief, I hate banana cake. And suddenly people seem to crave for sourdough bread! Is there a connection?'

'Making a decent living is better than free-loading from these food banks.'

'Aiyo! So, depressing. No more talk of politics and Covid. Let's get back to talking about sex.'

'Crazy, lah, you. Anyway, did I tell you what Jack gave me as my birthday gift?'

'Hang on. There's a message coming in on my mobile phone.'

Surin read the message on his phone. He suddenly had a worried look. He read the message again. He remembered that Deva was still on the line.

'Hei, that was the Exora guy.' Surin voice had lost all its light-heartedness.

'What's wrong? You sound like you heard of another Covid death.'

'The Exora guy sent me a message. He said he had tested positive for HIV. He said I should go a for a test too.'

Deva froze, the old fear from those days when 'HIV positive' was but a death sentence returned to him. He shook his head to wave those memories away, put on a brave front and said, 'Hei, Surin, sorry, that's tough. You did have safe sex, didn't you?'

'Fuck! I should have kept my dick under lock and key during this bloody lockdown. Now the bother and the stress.'

Surin put the handset on his phone cradle and stared at the last message on his mobile phone. Deva heard his phone go suddenly dead. He was not used to an abrupt end to a phone call with Surin. 'I'll call him tomorrow. Damn all these viruses,' he thought to himself. He poured himself a big shot of whiskey.

Acknowledgements

My sincere gratitude to all my readers who have supported my work since the first publication of my stories in 1995. Thank you to the late Jeremy Hunter, John McRae, and Danton Remoto for giving me your valuable time during the early drafts of my short stories.

My gratitude to John Lee and Law King Hui of Maya Press for publishing my work since 2016. To editors Kee Thuan Chye, Jose Varghese, Dipak Giri, Mitali Chakravarty, and Amir Muhammad for publishing my stories.

My love and gratitude to my sons, Vincent Jeremiah Edwin and Julian Matthew Edwin, and my companions, Too Wei Keong and Kayven Chew Kian Tatt, for always being there for me.

Previously Published

1. 'The Kiss' first appeared in *Sunday Style, The New Sunday Times*, 19 March 1995.
2. 'Husband Material' was first published in *The Literary Page, The New Straits Times*, May 1996.
3. 'The Best Man's Kiss' first appeared in the online journal *Lakeview International Journal of Literature and Arts*, Vol. 5, No. 2, 2017.
4. 'Give Us This Day' first appeared in the 25 November 2018 online edition of the *Business Mirror*, Philippines.
5. 'Road Trip' first appeared in the online journal *Creative Flight Literary Journal*, Vol. 1, Issue 2, 2020.
6. 'Sleeping Demon' first appeared in the online journal *Queer Southeast Asia Literary Journal*, November Issue, 2020.
7. 'Brother Felix's Ward' first appeared in the online journal *Borderless*, August Issue, 2021.

8. 'The Desired One' first appeared in *The Big Book of Malaysian Horror Stories* in 2022 published by Fixi Novo.

9. Earlier versions of some of my stories first appeared in my collection titled *Coitus Interruptus and Other Stories* in 2018 published by Maya Press.